This book belongs
to

PUFFIN BOOKS

THE WORST WITCH

AND THE WISHING STAR

Jill Murphy started putting books together (literally with a stapler) when she was six. Her Worst Witch series, the first book of which was published in 1974, is hugely successful. She has also written and illustrated several award-winning picture books for younger children.

Books by Jill Murphy

THE WORST WITCH

THE WORST WITCH STRIKES AGAIN

A BAD SPELL FOR THE WORST WITCH

THE WORST WITCH ALL AT SEA

THE WORST WITCH SAVES THE DAY

THE WORST WITCH TO THE RESCUE

THE WORST WITCH AND THE WISHING STAR

DEAR HOUND

THE WORST WITCH

WITCH

AND THE
WISHING STAR

JILL MURPHY

PUFFIN

PUFFIN BOOKS

UK | USA | Canada | Ireland | Australia
India | New Zealand | South Africa

Puffin Books is part of the Penguin Random House group of companies
whose addresses can be found at global.penguinrandomhouse.com

www.penguin.co.uk
www.puffin.co.uk
www.ladybird.co.uk

First published 2013
This edition published 2016

008

Copyright © Jill Murphy, 2013

The moral right of the author/illustrator has been asserted

Set in Baskerville
Printed and bound in Great Britain by Clays Ltd, Elcograf S.p.A.

A CIP catalogue record for this book is available from the British Library

ISBN: 978-0-141-37687-5

All correspondence to:
Puffin Books
Penguin Random House Children's
80 Strand, London WC2R ORL

MIX
Paper from
responsible sources
FSC
www.fsc.org   FSC® C018179

Penguin Random House is committed to a
sustainable future for our business, our readers
and our planet. This book is made from Forest
Stewardship Council® certified paper.

THE
WORST WITCH
AND THE WISHING STAR

CHAPTER ONE

Squalling rain and a biting wind buffeted the pupils of Miss Cackle's Academy as they struggled to reach the school in time for the first day of the Winter Term. The girls' cloaks kept blowing inside out, then flapping round their faces like wet flannels, and most of the older pupils (who were expected to keep the cats sitting on their brooms at all times) had given up and crammed the cats into their baskets for safety.

Mildred Hubble, who was *not* one of the best fliers in the school, was valiantly trying her best to keep Tabby (her nervous striped cat) perched on the broom just in case anyone was watching when she arrived. She had wedged Tabby between her back and a laundry-bag stuffed with books, and she could feel his claws through her gymslip as the unruly cloak flapped and whirled above her shoulders.

'Ouch!' she yelled. 'It's all right, Tab, we're nearly there . . . hang on just a teeny bit longer – OW! I didn't mean *literally* hang on! OW! OUCH!'

Mildred was quite right to be careful; someone *was* watching. Miss Cackle, their kindly headmistress, and Miss Hardbroom, her ferocious second-in-command, were lurking just out of sight in Miss Cackle's study, watching from the window as the girls wobbled or zoomed (depending on the gusting wind) over the wall and into the concrete playground.

'Well, just look at that, Miss Hardbroom,' exclaimed Miss Cackle. 'Mildred Hubble is the only senior pupil to have her cat *on* the broom, as stated in the regulations.'

'Hmmm,' said Miss Hardbroom. 'Don't

get *too* excited, Miss Cackle, I'm sure she'll manage some little disaster before too long – she usually does.'

'Now, now, Miss Hardbroom,' chided Miss Cackle. 'It's the first day of term and we must begin it with hope in our hearts – even when contemplating one of our more challenging pupils!'

Down in the windswept courtyard Miss Bat and Miss Mould were huddling beneath a huge dripping umbrella in the shelter of

the castle wall, directing the pupils to put any free-roaming cats into their baskets, leave everything in the cloakrooms and go straight to the Great Hall, as it was obviously far too wet to assemble in the playground. As usual, the first-years (who seemed smaller with each passing year to Mildred and her friends) arrived on foot, looking bedraggled and terrified as they entered the prison-like school and heard the gate clang shut behind them.

To the flying pupils' horror, the playground was full of puddles, so that the relief of arriving in one piece was ruined as the girls swooped and hovered, desperately trying to avoid landing in the water. One of the first rules of broomstick management is that brooms are badly affected if they are too near the surface of a large amount of water, which can make them stop working abruptly, and the last thing that anyone wanted was to crash-land in a puddle on the very first day.

Mildred was delighted to land safely, well clear of a deep puddle to her left. She jumped off and commanded the broom to wait and hover while she reached round and detached Tabby, claw by claw, from his rucksack-like position under her cloak. She shoved him back on to the broom next to the laundry-bag just in time to grab her best friend Maud, who had made it safely over the wall but was now heading for a small lake along the edge of the playground.

Maud was completely tangled up in her cloak and Mildred managed to catch her in the nick of time.

'Hold on, Maud!' yelled Mildred, flinging an arm round Maud's waist and restraining the broom with the other. 'Tell it to stop or you'll end up in that huge puddle!'

'Stay, broom!' shrieked Maud, unwrapping the cloak from her head and seizing her best friend in a bear hug. 'Thank goodness you saw me, Mil – you saved my bacon.'

Unfortunately they were not quick enough to save their friend Enid, who lurched suddenly over the wall in an uncontrollable nosedive straight into the lake of water which Maud had managed to avoid.

'Oh *no*!' cried Enid, spraying a plume of water behind her as she collapsed into

a messy heap of bags and cat basket, with her cloak billowing up around her on the surface of the puddle. 'Now everything's ruined – just look at it all!'

Enid's cat, who was locked in the basket, was yowling his head off as the water seeped in round his paws. The broomstick was floating in the water, looking as if it would never do anything magic again, and Enid, though trying to keep calm, had burst into tears. Mildred and Maud helped Enid to her feet and dragged all her luggage clear of the huge puddle as quickly as possible.

'It's all right, Enid,' said Maud reassuringly, wringing out the hem of her friend's dripping cloak. 'It's not as bad as it looks and your broom will be fine as soon as it's dried out.'

'Hey, you two!' said Mildred suddenly. 'Nice to see you again!' She held her arms out and the three best friends flung their arms round each other and jumped about in the rain – unexpectedly pleased, despite the horrible weather and the long Winter Term ahead, that they were back together again, come what may.

CHAPTER TWO

Mildred couldn't help feeling secretly thrilled that *she* wasn't the one squelching and dripping up the stairs as they made their way from the cloakrooms to the Great Hall. If anyone made a dramatic entrance to Miss Cackle's on the first day of term it was usually Mildred, and she felt grateful for her perfect landing, especially in front of all those juniors, blowing around the playground like dustbin lids on a windy rubbish day.

'Do you think anyone saw?' asked Enid anxiously, wringing the last drops of water from her long, thick plait.

'I don't honestly think it matters too much,' said Maud kindly. 'People were plummeting into puddles all over the place, especially the younger ones – they can't give the entire school a detention in the first five minutes!'

'Maud's right,' agreed Mildred, feeling happy to be in the unusual position of offering comfort to someone else. 'It's not *our* fault that the school's on top of a mountain; the weather's nearly always doing something horrible up here – do you remember once when there was a blizzard on the first day of Summer Term?'

'And it was a day like this,' continued Maud, 'when Mildred rescued her tortoise from the top of the pine tree outside the school gates. Gales and rain are part of the deal up here, Enid, no one will give a hoot about anyone in particular on such a ghastly first day.'

'Did you notice anything unusual in the playground?' asked Mildred, changing the subject. 'We were all so busy trying not to crash that it's only just dawned on me.'

'Not really,' said Maud. 'Everything looked the same as ever. What was it?'

'I've just realized that Miss Drill wasn't there,' continued Mildred. 'She's always the first person you see when you arrive, standing there in her gym kit, bossing

everyone about and shepherding the new arrivals, but this time it was Miss Bat and Mouldy.' (Mouldy was the girls' nickname for Miss Mould, the art mistress.)

'Perhaps she's not well,' suggested Enid. 'Or she might have retired – she looks quite old.'

'They *all* look quite old,' commented Mildred. 'I don't think Miss Drill is older than anyone else – anyway, it doesn't really matter *where* she is. We only have her for gym three or four times a week – all those broomstick exercise routines and cross-country runs, euch!'

'Perhaps we'll get a new gym mistress,' said Enid.

'A new one might be worse!' said Maud. 'She might be young and keen.'

'Or older and more crotchety!' laughed Mildred.

They had reached the doors of the Great Hall, which were propped open so that the girls could pass inside more quickly.

Mildred linked arms with her two best friends. 'Here we go again,' she said. 'Time to find out what's in store for us *this* year.'

CHAPTER THREE

The first thing that Mildred noticed as the new Form Four shuffled into line and glanced up at the teachers' platform was Miss Drill, dressed in a grey tweed suit and a purple blouse, her wavy grey hair scragged into an untidy French pleat instead of her usual jaunty ponytail.

'Look at Miss Drill!' whispered Mildred to Maud. 'I've never seen her out of shorts – doesn't it look strange to see her in a proper outfit?'

'Enough chatting, girls!' warned Miss Hardbroom. 'Get into your places at once! You've had long enough to greet each other and calm down after your *extremely* disorderly arrival – don't think I didn't notice the *puddle* incident, Enid Nightshade – *not* a very good start, even if the weather *has* been a trifle extreme.'

Enid closed her eyes as if in pain.

'Welcome back, girls,' beamed Miss Cackle, taking over hastily from her second-in-command before the whole school was plunged into a state of terrified misery. 'I'm sure the dreadful weather hasn't been much help to any of us! Not to worry, there are many exciting new announcements to warm your hearts on this first day of the Winter Term, including a brilliant opportunity for one lucky witches' school – and I sincerely hope it will be *this* one – to win a new *indoor* swimming pool.'

There were gasps of delighted amazement from the girls.

'There now!' continued Miss Cackle, clapping her hands together gleefully, like a little girl. 'I *knew* that would cheer you all up!'

'I thought we were saving that piece of information until the end of all the other announcements!' muttered Miss Hardbroom.

'Oh dear, Miss Hardbroom,' mumbled Miss Cackle. 'You're quite right – as usual. I'm afraid I got a bit carried away – I've been longing to tell the girls all about it. Perhaps you could take over and –'

'Certainly,' said Miss Hardbroom crisply. 'Now then, girls, there are several new things to tell you about. First of all, Miss Drill has decided to give up her position as gym mistress, due to a knee injury sustained during her annual rock-climbing summer holiday. Not wishing to lose such a dedicated teacher, we have persuaded Miss Drill to stay on as class teacher to this year's Form Four. We are trying hard to find a new gym mistress for later in the term, so Form Four can count themselves lucky that Miss Drill will be able to keep them fit and healthy until gym classes are up and running again.'

Maud and Enid glanced sideways at Mildred, who was looking desperate.

'During the holidays,' said Miss Hardbroom, 'there have been exciting improvements in all the bedrooms. Glass has been fitted in every pupil's window.'

There were whoops of joy from the entire school, except the bewildered first-years, who had no idea that their bedrooms would not have had proper windows in the first place; but there was great rejoicing from all the old hands as they imagined snuggling up in a cosy bed, without rain and wind blowing on to their pillows. In particularly bad weather, they had all had to move their beds away from the open stone windows.

'Settle down now, girls!' barked Miss Hardbroom. 'What is it, Mildred?'

Mildred had put up her hand.

'Excuse me, Miss Hardbroom,' she began shyly, as everyone turned to look at her. 'I was just wondering how the bats are going to get in and out.'

Miss Cackle smiled and put a staying hand on Miss Hardbroom's arm to show that she would answer the question.

'I *knew* you'd be anxious about that, Mildred,' said Miss Cackle. 'Don't worry, my dear, we've put a small swinging flap on each window – a sort of bat flap, you might say – we've already checked and they've obviously got used to the idea. The usual furry flock was huddled along your picture rail when I last looked.'

'Thank you, Miss Cackle,' said Mildred, breathing a sigh of relief.

'Would you like to carry on with the final announcement, Miss Cackle?' asked Miss Hardbroom, sounding a little tetchy. 'Or shall I?'

'Actually, Miss Hardbroom,' said Miss Cackle, feeling braver than usual, 'I think *I* will, if you don't mind.'

'Of course I don't,' said Miss Hardbroom primly. 'You *are* the headmistress, Miss Cackle.'

'Well then, girls!' said Miss Cackle, looking quite radiant. 'This brings me to the swimming-pool competition, and not just *any* old outdoor, freezing-cold swimming pool but an *in*door one, to be used all year round. Such a magnificent prize – goodness me, we will all be *so* fit –'

'We have to actually *win* the competition first, Miss Cackle,' said Miss Hardbroom sourly, 'which will mean *weeks* of diligent practice, not to mention coming up with a prize-winning idea in the first place.'

'Yes, of course, Miss Hardbroom,' said Miss Cackle. 'I was coming to that in a moment.'

'Not a moment too soon, if you ask *me*!' said Miss Hardbroom, her piercing gaze managing to convince every pupil that she was looking into their very soul. 'There will be a *great* deal of extra work involved in getting the competing pupils up to scratch if we are to be in the running for such a prize.'

'Thank you, Miss Hardbroom,' said Miss Cackle tactfully. 'I hope you were listening, girls! The competition is between all the witches' schools in the country and we have some *very* stiff competition, especially as there seem to be new schools for sorcery popping up like mushrooms these days. Miss Pentangle's Academy is a strong contender and Moonridge High School is also doing rather well. The details of the competition are to be found on the noticeboard in the passageway next to the cloakrooms, to be discussed with your form teachers tomorrow. Also there, you will find the lists giving certain selected pupils their form tasks. Read them well – we expect any pupil lucky enough to have been chosen, to take her task seriously, to ensure the smooth running of everyday life at Miss Cackle's Academy, the best witches' academy in the land!'

Miss Cackle smiled happily down at her girls, who all realized that they could risk cheering and looking happy for a brief moment, before Miss Hardbroom brought them back down to earth.

'To conclude!' said Miss Hardbroom, motioning to the girls to be silent. 'You may spend the next few hours drying out your clothes and tending to your cats in your rooms. First-years, stay behind and I will explain the rules so that you will know where you cannot go and what you are not allowed to do. Miss Bat?'

Miss Bat the chanting mistress, who was beginning to look more scruffily vague with each passing year, seated herself at the ancient piano and began to play a stirring piece of music. Mildred would never have admitted it but the strident rhythm of the piano lifted her spirits as she marched her way out of the Great Hall and into the new term.

CHAPTER FOUR

'**L**et's go and check out the tasks,' said Maud as they clattered down the stairs.

'I think we get more difficult stuff, now that we're in Form Four,' said Enid gloomily.

'Well *I* hope I haven't got anything at *all*,' said Mildred.

'Hello, you three,' said someone coming up behind them, draping an arm round Mildred and Maud's shoulders.

'Oh hello, Ethel,' said Mildred, turning to see that it was indeed Ethel, her least favourite person. 'We were just wondering what our tasks might be.'

'I hope I've got First-Year Mentor,' said Ethel. 'They're all so gullible and it would be brilliant scaring the wits out of them and sending them off on the wrong errands.'

'That's not very nice, Ethel,' said Enid. 'Anyway, they'll want someone kind and helpful as their mentor, not a meanie like you, and H.B. knows what you're like after you pinched Mildred's project last term.'

'That was just a silly misunderstanding,' snapped Ethel. 'She didn't need to make such a stupid fuss about it – it was only a joke that got out of hand.'

'No it wasn't!' exclaimed Mildred indignantly. 'H.B. caught you fair and square, so you'll have to watch what you're doing from now on – just like the rest of us.'

'Oh, keep your hair on,' snapped Ethel. 'You always get in such a *state* about everything.'

They had reached the passageway where

the list of tasks was pinned up on a long noticeboard. There was already a large crowd of girls pushing and jostling and standing on tiptoe, trying to see if their names were on the list.

'I *really* hope I haven't been chosen for anything,' said Mildred, keeping her fingers tightly crossed.

'Don't worry, Mil,' said Maud, giving her friend's hand a squeeze. 'You'll probably get Blackboard Monitor. Even a first-year could rub out the last lesson, ready for the next.'

Meanwhile, Miss Cackle was sitting in the staffroom having a cup of tea and a macaroon with Miss Hardbroom.

'I do hope we've done the right thing, choosing Mildred for the East Wing Lantern Monitor,' said Miss Cackle, dipping the macaroon into the tea, holding it there until it was just about to dissolve, then hastily popping it into her mouth. 'It's quite a big responsibility for such a scatterbrain and she's always been a bit scared of the dark.'

'Nonsense, Miss Cackle,' said Miss Hardbroom. 'It's not as if she's been given the entire school. She'll just have three corridors of bedrooms, the spiral stairs, passages to the cloakrooms, the hallway inside the main door and the two large lanterns on the school gates. As long as she sets off at twilight and lights her way out to the gates, everything will be shining brightly to light her back in again.'

'You make it sound so simple, Miss Hardbroom,' said Miss Cackle, who had misjudged the macaroon-dipping and dropped a glutinous lump down her front. 'Oh dear, what a mess I've made.' She removed it with a handkerchief, inadvertently crushing it into her dress, and put what remained of it into her saucer. 'I suppose you're right, Miss Hardbroom.

29

Which girls are doing the West Wing and all the upper floors?'

'Ethel Hallow and Drusilla Paddock,' said Miss Hardbroom. 'So at least two-thirds of the school will be efficiently lit. Anyway, I've made sure they each have a bag full of safety equipment to take with them, so please don't worry yourself, headmistress. All will be well.'

'I sincerely hope so, Miss Hardbroom,' sighed Miss Cackle. 'Perhaps Mildred will be *glad* of the responsibility, now that she's a senior pupil.'

CHAPTER FIVE

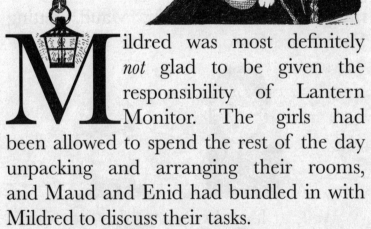

Mildred was most definitely *not* glad to be given the responsibility of Lantern Monitor. The girls had been allowed to spend the rest of the day unpacking and arranging their rooms, and Maud and Enid had bundled in with Mildred to discuss their tasks.

'It's not fair,' said Mildred, sitting huddled on her bed with Tabby and her two friends. 'I bet H.B. did it on purpose.'

'It's not actually *that* bad,' said Enid reassuringly. 'You've only got the East

Wing and the playground. If you set off just before it gets dark and light your way out, it'll be nice and bright when you come back in again.'

'Anyway,' grumbled Mildred, 'I'll have to get up at dawn to go round and douse all the candles, so while you're all slumbering in your warm beds, I'll be freezing to death going round all those creepy corridors by myself – you're so lucky, Maud, getting First-Year Mentor.'

'Well, at least I've saved the little dears from Ethel's clutches,' laughed Maud. 'She and Drusilla are Lantern Monitors for the rest of the school.'

'What exactly *is* First-Year Mentor?' asked Enid.

'Just keeping an eye on the first-years,' said Maud. 'Making sure no one's *too* homesick etc. They all look such babies, don't they? Do you remember how *we* felt when we first arrived?'

'Everything went wrong every five seconds,' said Mildred.

'Tell Enid about the dustbin incident, Mil,' said Maud. 'She wasn't here when it happened – she didn't come until the Summer Term.'

'I think I'd rather not,' said Mildred gloomily.

'Oh, go on, Millie,' encouraged Enid. 'Please tell!'

'Well,' said Mildred, 'we were having our very first flying lesson on the second day and I got a bit over-confident and crashed into the dustbins and broke my broom. It's been the same ever since really, one disaster after another.'

'Not *all* the time,' said Maud in her usual cheery way. 'You've done loads of *good* things, Millie – I'm not quite sure *how* exactly, but things often go wonderfully right in the end for you, even if it's usually the long way round.'

'Well, I'd like the *short* way round this time,' said Mildred. 'Did you get a task, Enid?'

'Flower Monitor,' said Enid. 'You know, beautifying the classroom. It says that I have to use my initiative and find sprays of berried leaves and pine cones if there aren't any actual flowers at this time of year.'

Just at that moment, the bats, who had been hanging upside down along the picture rail, snuffling and quivering in their sleep, began waking up and stretching their wings in the darkening room. Fortunately,

Mildred's task didn't start until the following night, making this her last free evening until the next school holidays. There were now eight bats in Mildred's room, forming a good-sized colony, and the girls watched fascinated as they headed for the newly glazed window, neatly nudging the bat flap open with their grey furry heads one by one, and disappearing into the twilight.

'How amazing!' said Mildred. 'I really thought they wouldn't like using the bat flap – you know how well they avoid bashing into things with their radar.'

'It's finally stopped raining,' said Maud, peering out of the window. 'The sky's completely cleared and you can see the stars beginning to twinkle.'

'Oh look, Maud!' exclaimed Mildred. 'There's a shooting star – over there behind the gates – it sort of tumbled down the sky.'

'Quick, Mildred!' said Enid. 'Make a wish – and don't tell us what it is or it won't come true.'

'And be careful what you wish for!' warned Maud.

Mildred closed her eyes and wished.

CHAPTER SIX

The teachers had gathered in the staffroom to deal with the problems that always needed ironing out on the first day back. It was also an opportune moment to have a calming cup of tea and a biscuit – or several biscuits in Miss Cackle's case.

'Everything seems to be running smoothly, Miss Cackle,' said Miss Bat, dropping a handful of teabags into an enormous teapot. 'Though I must say, Miss Drill, you were sorely missed helping with the first-years, especially in such dreadful weather.'

'I quite missed them myself,' said Miss Drill, re-pinning a fallen clump of her springy hair, 'though I *am* looking forward to being class teacher to Form Four. Luckily, I'll have Ethel Hallow to get things off to a good start.'

'*Un*luckily, you'll also have Mildred Hubble,' said Miss Hardbroom drily. 'So goodness knows what will be waiting round the corner.'

'Look, everyone!' said Miss Cackle, swiftly changing the subject. 'The horrible weather's completely changed – the sky is so clear now, you can even see the stars coming out.'

Miss Hardbroom craned her neck and peered out into the gathering gloom. 'Did you see that?' she said. 'A shooting star just zipped across the sky, over there behind the gates.'

'You must make a wish!' exclaimed Miss Cackle. 'Quickly, Miss Hardbroom, or it

38

won't come true.'

'Oh really, Miss Cackle,' said Miss Hardbroom grumpily. 'Surely you don't believe in all that silly nonsense?'

'It is *not* silly nonsense,' replied Miss Cackle indignantly. 'Didn't you ever make a birthday wish when you blew out the candles on your cake?'

'We didn't *have* birthday candles in our house,' said Miss Hardbroom, sounding briefly wistful. 'Or cakes, or cards, or anything frivolous *and* we only had one present – usually something useful, such as a new spell book; not like nowadays, when they have so many presents that they need a fork-lift truck to get them all home.'

The other teachers .stared at Miss Hardbroom, imagining her as a child in a sensible black party dress, clutching her one present to her chest. It suddenly explained a great deal about her character.

'Come along now, Miss Hardbroom,' continued Miss Cackle brightly. 'Make a wish anyway, just to prove it one way or another.'

'Oh yes, Miss Hardbroom,' giggled Miss Bat. 'That would be such fun! *Do* make a wish.'

'All right then,' said Miss Hardbroom,

feeling unexpectedly caught up in the spirit of fun and camaraderie between her fellow teachers. 'If it means so much to all of you.'

'You have to close your eyes,' said Miss Cackle.

'And don't tell us what you've wished,' said Miss Drill. 'Or it won't come true.'

Miss Hardbroom closed her eyes and wished. After a few seconds, she opened one eye and glanced at her fellow teachers. 'What do I do next?' she asked earnestly.

'Nothing at all, Miss Hardbroom!' said Miss Cackle, stifling a smile.

'Oh,' said Miss Hardbroom, feeling a little disappointed, as she had rather hoped for some sort of magic to accompany the wish.

'Right then, ladies,' she continued primly, her sense of fun departing as suddenly as it had arrived. 'Enough silly nonsense. We have a *very* arduous term in front of us and only hard work and planning can keep us ahead of all the other schools if we want to win this competition.'

CHAPTER SEVEN

ext morning, Mildred was already awake when the rising bell clanged through the corridors. She had hardly had any sleep, mainly because the bats had been in and out of the bat flap all night. It made a clunking rattle each time one of them came in or went out, and as there were now eight of them, the flap was clunking and rattling the whole night long. To make matters worse, Tabby jumped out of his skin every time the bat flap crashed open and Mildred had to give him extra cuddles to calm him

down. The bats had all finally come back in to roost along the picture rail, but it was too late for Mildred, who had only slept for about two hours altogether.

Maud put her head round the door, already in her uniform. 'Up you get, Mil,' she said cheerfully. '*Oh* dear, what's up? You look awful.'

'The bats have been driving me mad,' said Mildred, yawning and stretching. 'They were in and out like a fiddler's elbow all night long. I know it's nice to have glass in the windows, but I think I preferred it when there wasn't any. I never heard a thing in the old days – *and* it disturbs Tabby.'

'I haven't got any bats at all in my room,' said Maud, 'so I was OK and I think Enid's only got two. Never mind, Mil, you'll soon get used to it. My auntie lives right next door to a railway line and the walls shake every time a train zooms past. When you first stay there it makes you jump every time it happens and you lie there waiting for the next one, but after a while you really don't notice; it's the same with chiming clocks – my auntie's got one of those too! Where's Einstein, by the way? Did you bring him with you?'

Einstein was the tortoise that Mildred had used for her animal transformation spell the term before and Miss Cackle had allowed her to keep him.

'He's gone into early hibernation,' said Mildred. 'He's under the bed in the cat basket, tucked up in a blanket.'

She clambered out of bed and rooted around in her wardrobe for a shirt and her gymslip.

'I do *like* the bats, Maudie,' she yawned, 'and it *is* less absolutely freezing with the new glass, but I sometimes wish the school was more *normal*.'

'I know just what you mean,' agreed Maud. 'Any other school would be thrilled because they were getting some vital new piece of equipment, but *we're* all delirious with joy because they've finally put glass in the windows. It's like the Middle Ages at Miss Cackle's.'

'Don't you sometimes sneakily wish we'd been sent to Pentangle's?' asked Mildred thoughtfully. 'They've got lovely purple uniforms and the head girl gets to choose any type of cat she wants. The head girl at the moment's got a beautiful cream and brown Ragdoll cat – not that I'd want to change Tabby!' she added hastily. 'Anyway, there wouldn't be much chance of my being the head girl of *any* school so it's not worth worrying about.'

'Cackle's is all right really,' said Maud, trying to think the best, as usual. 'It may not be very modern, but it gets there in the end and, anyway, *we* wouldn't have met each other if we weren't both here! Come on, grab your tie, and here's your sash round the bedpost, and let's go and see if Enid's ready.'

Mildred smiled sleepily and felt a peaceful glow of happiness that someone as nice as Maud had chosen to be her friend.

CHAPTER EIGHT

Miss Drill was deeply delighted with her new position as form teacher. She was waiting for Form Four on the platform at the front of the classroom half an hour early, wearing a dark green suit with a lilac shirt and a purple tie with yellow stars emblazoned all over it. She was so excited about being in proper clothes, instead of her customary shorts, Aertex shirt and black fleece if it was chilly, that her sense of taste had rather deserted her. Trying to fit in as many colours as possible, without deviating too far from the traditional dark colours, had proved tricky. However, Miss Drill had gazed at herself approvingly in her long mirror that morning and felt confident and fashionable. 'Yes,' she thought to herself, 'I look quite . . . *trendy*. I think the girls will be *most* impressed.'

The girls *were* impressed when they filed into their new classroom after breakfast, but not quite in the way that Miss Drill had hoped for.

'Settle down now, girls,' said Miss Drill. 'I don't know what is causing all this giggling and silliness.'

Enid and Maud were staring desperately at the floor, neither of them daring to look at Mildred, whose shoulders were beginning to shake as she tried to focus on anything but Miss Drill's almost fluorescent tie. They all managed to pull themselves together after arranging their books and writing equipment in their desks and they were soon all sitting up straight, politely awaiting their instructions for the day.

'Good morning, girls,' said Miss Drill, an excited catch in her voice as she spoke.

'Good *morn*ing, Miss Drill,' chorused the girls in that sing-song way used by schools everywhere.

'First of all,' announced Miss Drill, 'I promised Miss Hardbroom that I would give out the essential equipment to all three of our Lantern Monitors. Come up here, Ethel, Drusilla and Mildred.'

Miss Drill handed each of them a surprisingly large canvas holdall, which contained a fire blanket, a fire extinguisher, several boxes of candles, a box of tapers, a box of matches, a large lantern with a clip on the side for a taper and a special handle (a bit like one of those holders for coffee glasses), so that the monitor could easily dip in a taper to light all the lanterns, and a snuffer for dousing the candles in the morning.

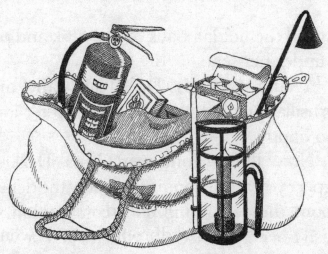

'Miss Hardbroom asked me to make it clear to the Lantern Monitors that she will be expecting them to commence their duties at twilight this evening,' said Miss Drill. 'Make sure you leave yourselves plenty of time, and you should take your brooms with you, as some of the lanterns – and candelabras – are quite high and you will need to fly up to light them. You may also keep your broomsticks in your rooms, as you will need them to hand. Oh, and you don't have to take the cats on lantern duty.'

'Yes, Miss Drill,' said Mildred, trying hard to remember the instructions as she lugged the holdall back to her desk and put it under her seat.

'Thank you, Miss Drill,' said Ethel and Drusilla together, though Ethel didn't look too happy.

'Now then,' continued Miss Drill. 'I expect you are all longing to know the details about the swimming-pool competition. It hasn't been decided yet which class or who in particular will be representing the school, but this competition is quite unusual as it is more of a talent competition than the usual formal display.'

The girls all perked up at this piece of news.

'I *thought* that would catch your interest,' said Miss Drill with a beaming smile. 'There will be one act representing each school and the judges are to be the Supreme Magician, the Grand High Witch and the Chief Wizard. The judges have stated that they want to be thoroughly entertained! The act can be anything at all, but the person or persons *must* have star quality – something that puts them above everyone else.'

'Excuse me, Miss Drill,' said Ethel, putting up her hand. 'Could we have a chanting choir?'

'Or a dance troupe!' exclaimed Enid.

'I'm not sure if Miss Hardbroom would approve of a dance troupe, Enid,' said Miss Drill, 'especially if it was one of those modern ones, with everyone leaping about in an abandoned fashion wearing leotards – and, of course, it has to be something to reflect our position as a witches' academy. A chanting choir sounds very suitable, Ethel. We'll have to put our thinking caps on, but before we do you can all run down to the broom sheds, fetch your broomsticks and fly three times round the school to wake yourselves up! I'll come down with you and time everyone with my stopwatch.'

There was a huge groan, which rippled round the class like thunder.

'Now, now, girls,' chirped Miss Drill. 'That is *not* the attitude! Look at the glorious day waiting for you out there, with a perfect rain-washed blue sky; it's just splendid after yesterday's storm clouds and there's a lovely light breeze to keep you on your toes, so to speak. Up you get and off you go – and don't forget to fetch your cats; I'm sure they could do with some exercise too.'

Miss Drill held out her arms and shooed them from the room like a large flock of unwilling geese.

CHAPTER NINE

'There doesn't seem to be much wrong with her knee, if you ask me,' grumbled Mildred to Maud as they hastened to collect their cats.

'I think she just pretended she'd hurt it, so that she could be a class teacher and keep out of the cold,' agreed Enid. 'Anyway, she seems even more exercise-mad than she used to be –'

'– as long as *we're* the ones doing the exercise,' commented Mildred mutinously.

'I still think it's better than another year of Miss Hardbroom,' said Maud. 'Miss Drill's always quite cheerful, even if she *is* going to wear us out!'

Tabby was appalled when Mildred roused him from his deep morning slumber on her pillow.

'It's no use, Tab,' said Mildred, scooping him up gently and carrying him yowling down the spiral stairs and out to the broom shed. '*I'm* not crazy about flying either, but we both have to do it.'

'Poor old Mildred,' sneered Ethel, already on her broom, with her cat, Nightstar, sitting behind her like an ebony statue. 'It must be so hard for you, stuck with that stripey weirdo – I mean, you're not a bad basic flier really; it's just that you look completely ridiculous with that *thing* doing its nut behind you. I can't imagine anyone's going to be rushing to put *you* in line for this competition. Maybe you'd stand a better chance if you pleaded with Miss Cackle to get you a better cat.'

Mildred held Tabby close to her chest, hoping that he hadn't understood what Ethel had said.

'There's no better cat than Tabby!' she said fiercely. 'Anyway, Miss Cackle *did* try to give me another cat once, ages ago, when she sent Tabby to be a kitchen mouser, and we were both so miserable that in the end she let me have him back.'

'Actually,' said Maud, 'they might not choose *anyone* from our class. It really *is* going to be whoever has the best idea.'

'And another thing, Mildred Hubble,' said Ethel, hovering alongside Mildred, who was trying to peel Tabby off her front. 'How come we get holdalls full of safety equipment as Lantern Monitors these days? It always *used* to be a jam jar with a candle and a taper. *I* think H.B. made sure we've got safety stuff because she knows you'll probably set the school on fire otherwise. It's so embarrassing, as well as heavy to lug around. You always manage to ruin everything before it's even started.'

At this point, Miss Drill joined them in the playground (having taken quite a long time to hobble down the spiral staircase). Happily for Mildred, this stopped Ethel from working herself up into a full-blown rant – Mildred could always tell when Ethel was gunning for her, as she started addressing her by both names.

'Right then, girls!' Miss Drill announced encouragingly. 'I want you all to line up so that you get a fair start and I'll time each lap. Don't go any higher than the third floor, watch out for turrets and there'll be a tin of caramel toffees for the person who's the fastest – I can't say fairer than that on this beautiful morning. Ready, steady, GO!'

CHAPTER TEN

ildred's first evening as Lantern Monitor approached at the speed of light – in fact, she had never known a double potions lesson go by so fast before.

'Isn't it strange,' she had mused to Maud at lunch-break, '*you* know – how time shoots past when you're *not* looking forward to something, like going to the dentist, but takes forever if you're waiting for something nice like a birthday party?'

Maud tapped on Mildred's door at

the end of the day and found her friend studying the map of all the corridors and stairs that had been assigned to her.

'Oh, hi, Maud,' said Mildred, trying to sound confident. 'Do you think it's dark enough to get started yet? I don't want to get stranded in a pitch-black corridor somewhere before I've lit everything.'

As if to answer her question, the first bat detached itself from the sleeping bat-huddle, nosed open the bat flap and set off hunting.

'I guess that answers my question!' laughed Mildred, picking up the holdall. 'Wish me luck.'

'Good luck, Millie,' said Maud. 'I'm just off myself, monitoring the first-years while they do their homework, so I'll see you later.'

'See you then,' said Mildred. 'Gosh, Maud, aren't we getting grown-up and responsible!'

Mildred lit the taper-lantern, hoisted the bag on to her broom and set off down the

corridor, the broom hovering obediently behind her like a well-trained dog. She soon got the hang of flipping open the little door at the side of each wall-lantern, lighting the candle with the taper and watching the golden glow spread along the walls and ceilings.

The light was failing by the time she reached the playground and the pine trees were beginning to look inky black and sinister outside the high prison-like walls.

'At least it's not raining,' she thought, trying not to be unnerved by the darkness.

Mildred lit the lanterns on the outside of the huge oak doors, which lit the way across to the playground gates. Then she saw something move – something lurking outside the gates, half-hidden in the gloom. Mildred could sense a presence out there, watching her.

'Don't be silly,' she scolded herself. 'It's just your imagination giving you the creeps.'

To reassure herself, Mildred held up the taper-lantern and to her horror she saw a pair of red glinting eyes staring back at her.

Her heart began to hammer as she lowered the lantern and kept perfectly still.

For a few minutes there was no sound at all, except her own heartbeat thudding in her ears, then she heard a low whimper – then another, then more and more, getting faster and faster, until they joined together in a chain of high-pitched yelping. Mildred could tell that it was the sound of an animal in distress and she began to feel curious instead of petrified. Cautiously, she approached the gates and held up the lantern again.

CHAPTER ELEVEN

It was a dog. A small, filthy, tatty, terrified dog, who leapt at the gates, scrabbling frantically, trying to push his nose through the bars and licking the air in a desperate attempt to make contact with her.

Mildred was astonished. The secret wish she had made on the shooting star was for a dog – only she hadn't meant *now*! She had sort of been hoping that it might appear on her birthday, or during the holidays – in fact, any time at all other than her first evening as Lantern Monitor!

'Shhh!' said Mildred, dropping to her knees and putting her hands through the bars so that she could smooth his fur and try to calm him down. 'Shh now! It's all right – I'll come over the gates and get you. *Do* stop yelping or someone'll come.'

Mildred left the holdall on the ground, took the taper-lantern with her and hovered up the inside of the gates and over the top. The little dog was hysterical with excitement and nearly knocked her off the broom as she hovered neatly down the other side and landed on the grass. *Very* carefully, Mildred put the taper-lantern to one side, sat down and allowed the dog to spring into her lap, frenziedly washing her beneath her chin and barking joyfully in her ear.

'Hey, that's enough, little dog!' she laughed, putting her arms round him and holding him off. He was very thin; Mildred could feel his ribs sticking out as she tried to restrain him. 'It's OK, little one, you'll be all right now; I've got you.'

For several minutes Mildred sat on the grass in the flickering lantern-light, smoothing and petting the grimy little animal. Gradually she calmed him down until he stopped yelping and scrabbling, finally settling into her lap with a comfortable-sounding doggy grunt.

'*Now* what?' thought Mildred. 'I can't just leave him here after all my promises to help him – especially as he's my wish come true! Perhaps I'd better take him back to my room before someone comes to check that I've done the lanterns properly.'

Mildred stood up, still holding the dog in her arms, and lowered him (fortunately, he was a very small dog with short, sturdy legs) on to the back of the broom. He sat very calmly and didn't try to jump off, so she picked up the taper-lantern and tried a ten-inch hover to see if he could cope with flying. The upward movement didn't seem to worry him at all – he even gave a little wag of his tail – so Mildred continued to hover up as smoothly as possible, pausing to light the outside lanterns, then inching her way very gently over the top of the gates and back down into the concrete playground.

To her surprise, the little dog just sat there on the broom, his head tilted slightly to one side, making no attempt to jump off.

68

Mildred glanced across the darkening yard up at the school windows, some of which were softly lit by candles. She rarely saw the school from the outside at night and was surprised how beautiful it looked, with its lantern-light and glowing windows. She could also make out several bats flitting in and out of the long shadows like clockwork flying toys.

It suddenly felt rather exciting to be out and about, being a responsible Lantern Monitor, having completed her task without mishap, and Mildred couldn't help feeling slightly irritated that she was now lumbered with an illicit animal that might get her into serious trouble on the first evening. She smoothed his grimy head and wondered how on earth she was going to sneak him up to her room.

The holdall came to her rescue. It was a large zipped bag with quite a lot of room inside, despite all the equipment stuffed into it.

'In you hop!' said Mildred, unzipping the bag, arranging the fire blanket on top of

the more uncomfortable items, such as the fire extinguisher, and patting the blanket invitingly.

The dog jumped in at once and Mildred re-zipped the bag, leaving it slightly open so that he could breathe. She heaved the holdall on to the back of the broom by its handles, and the broom dipped lower for a few seconds under the weight, then shifted back up to its usual hovering level.

'Just keep quiet,' whispered Mildred into the opening. 'Not a sound.'

Mildred blew out the taper and candle now that her task was completed, and retraced her steps across the yard, back along the warmly glowing corridors and up the spiral staircase into the welcoming sanctuary of her room.

CHAPTER TWELVE

Mildred had completely forgotten about Tabby, who was still out taking a stroll around the corridors when she arrived back. She had let him out just before setting off and had then become so wrapped up in the lantern-lighting and the dog that Tabby had slipped her mind.

Mildred hurried into the room, closed the door and lifted the holdall on to her bed, pulling back the zip so that the little dog could sit up and look round his new home. In spite of all the manic yelping and bustling when she had found him, he now seemed to be completely calm and sat up politely in the holdall awaiting instructions, gazing at Mildred as if she was the most wonderful sight he had ever seen. Mildred couldn't help feeling utterly charmed, especially when he solemnly gave her a paw.

'What a darling dog you are,' she said softly. 'You're a little star – and there's your name, "Star", just like the wishing star. What do you think? Is that a good name?'

Star gave an excited woof.

'No! No!' said Mildred, holding his jaws together. 'You can't bark in here – or anywhere, or I won't be allowed to keep you. They'll put you out again and you'll have to go back where you came from. I wonder where you *did* come from?'

She let go of his nose and he laid his muzzle into her hand.

Suddenly there was a knock at the door. 'Are you back yet, Mil?' called Enid's voice.

'It's all looking nice and brightly lit out here!' added Maud, who was obviously there too.

'Hang on a sec!' yelled Mildred, stuffing the holdall under the bed and plonking Star back inside it. '*Stay*,' she whispered as loudly as she dared. 'Don't move, OK? Not a sound.'

She stood up and looked back at the bed. There was no movement and it was mercifully dark under there, with only the one candle burning on the window sill.

Mildred opened the door a crack and Tabby shot in, rubbing round her ankles.

'Can we come in?' asked Enid.

'No!' replied Mildred, glancing back over her shoulder at Tabby, who had frozen, ears back, body fluffed out like a furry puffer fish, staring fixedly into the darkness under the bed.

'Why not?' said Maud. 'Are you all right, Mil? Has something happened?'

'No!' exclaimed Mildred, smiling a little too brightly. 'It was all fine. I'm just a bit

75

tired. I thought I might go to bed early.'

'Not *this* early surely!' laughed Enid. 'Don't you want to hear about Maud and the first-years' homework? Is Tabby OK, Mil?'

Tabby was still in exactly the same position, now emitting the low whining growl that cats make when upset.

'He's fine,' said Mildred, smiling even more unnaturally. 'He's been a bit funny all day – haven't you, Tab?' She lunged into the room and grabbed him. 'It takes him ages to get over the long journey, doesn't it, Tabs?'

Tabby lurched over Mildred's shoulder and spat angrily in the direction of the bed.

'I really *am* going to bed early,' said Mildred, struggling to hang on to Tabby, who was trying to writhe out of her grasp. 'I've got to get up at the crack of dawn – literally – and I mustn't oversleep! Night then! Don't have any fun without me!'

'Night then, Mil,' said Maud, sounding a little crestfallen, as she was feeling rather

proud of her first real duty helping the first-years and had been looking forward to telling Mildred all about it.

'See you in the –' began Enid, but Mildred had closed the door.

'Sorry, Enid!' she called from the other side. 'I just don't want Tabs to get out. I can't think what's wrong with him.'

'Something's up,' said Maud as they made their way back to their own rooms.

'Perhaps she really *is* tired,' suggested Enid. 'I mean, she *does* have to get up early to put out the lanterns and Tabby's obviously in a state about *some*thing. Maybe she'll feel better about it all by tomorrow evening.'

'No,' said Maud. 'It isn't the lanterns. I *know* Mildred and something's up.'

Tabby was now perched on the bed rail, saucer-eyed and whining angrily. Mildred clicked her fingers and whispered to Star.

'Come on, Star. Come on, boy, out you come.' And out he came, hesitant and slightly cringing, for he could tell that the stripey cat was not pleased to see him. Mildred picked

Star up and placed him very gently on the bed, where he politely lay down wagging his tail. Tabby doubled to twice his size and let out a volley of hissing spits. Mildred had never heard him sound so angry.

'Oh, Tab,' she said, leaning towards him, 'you're still my best cat.' But he hissed at her and jumped on top of the wardrobe with his ears slicked back so tightly that he looked as if he didn't have any.

Eventually, feeling safe, high up above any danger, he began to blink and doze and his ears gradually lifted back to their usual position.

Mildred decided to get into bed and read. Star couldn't believe his luck when she gave him a bowl of Tabby's crunchy catfood on the bed, then let him curl up for the night on top of the covers.

She smoothed his head and a shower of dried mud fell on to the bedspread. 'I'll have to give you a wash and brush up tomorrow,' she laughed.

'Come on, Tabs,' she called to the shadow at the top of the wardrobe where she could just see the end of his tail, 'you've still got your place on my pillow. He's a really *nice* dog, Tabs. He won't hurt you. I just know it.'

But the only reply from Tabby was one last low growl before Mildred blew out the candle and settled down for a night of anxiety, hoping that the two of them wouldn't do anything that was going to end in a noisy argument.

CHAPTER THIRTEEN

It seemed as if Mildred had only been asleep for ten minutes when the alarm clock shrilled in her ear. Star leapt up and began barking and Mildred grabbed his snout and held on until he had fully woken up.

'You've got to be *so* quiet,' she whispered to him, gently releasing his nose. 'Come on, into the bag and you can come with me for a run around outside the gates.'

Mildred was dressed and ready as the grey morning light crept into the room. It was bitterly cold, despite the new glass, so she put on two cardigans over her uniform, which seemed a safer option than the voluminous cloak when handling candles.

Tabby was still on top of the wardrobe. She could see his glinting eyes glued to the holdall.

Mildred set off down the deserted corridors, flipping open the lanterns and dousing the candles as she went. It was so much easier than lighting them and, as the candles were all new, there would be

another few days before she had to replace them.

It was odd being the only one out in the deserted corridors. Every now and then one of the pupils' black cats came slinking past on its way back to its owner's room after a night's hunting.

Most of the cats stayed out all night and Tabby was unusual in spending the whole night on Mildred's bed. He stayed in as much as possible because the other cats bullied him.

'Poor Tab,' thought Mildred as she doused the large lantern above the main door, pulled back the bolts and stepped out into the playground. 'No wonder he's scared of our little newcomer.'

Mildred hovered up over the gates, doused the candles and landed behind the high wall out of sight of the windows in case anyone was looking. She just *knew* Miss Hardbroom would be on the prowl and that she needed to be extremely careful if she was going to keep her new pet a secret.

Mildred opened the holdall, lifted Star out and emptied the bowl of dried catfood that she had brought for his breakfast on to the grass.

The little dog bolted it down in seconds and wagged his tail gratefully. He had been lost in the woods for a long time and his previous owner had not been kind to him, and he could see that Mildred was the owner he had dreamed of. He was as bright as the wishing star he was named after and was determined to make his new mistress proud, bearing it bravely when Mildred produced a flask of water, flannel and a bar of soap, and gave him a thorough wash.

Mildred had been right to keep an eye out for Miss Hardbroom, who was at that very moment in the staffroom, watching Mildred's progress from the window.

She turned as the staffroom door opened and Miss Drill came in, clad in a purple and dark green zigzag striped dress with a rather garish lime-green cardigan. Miss Hardbroom winced.

'Oh, good morning, Miss Hardbroom,' said Miss Drill. 'I thought *I* was the first one up.'

'It seems that Mildred Hubble is the first one up today,' said Miss Hardbroom. 'She's even beaten Ethel and Drusilla, who are still toiling round the East Wing. I have to admit,' she added grudgingly, 'she really does seem to be taking her duties seriously.

I checked the lanterns last night and they were burning brightly, with all the lantern doors completely closed. It seems that being in a fine old establishment like Miss Cackle's Academy has finally rubbed off on our young misfit.'

'Well, *I've* had no trouble from her,' said Miss Drill. 'Would you like a nice cup of tea, Miss Hardbroom?'

'That would be just the ticket, Miss Drill,' said Miss Hardbroom, feeling somewhat relieved that the term had got off to such a calm and orderly start. 'Well, Miss Drill, we'd better sit down and work out a way to find the perfect "act", for want of a better word, to give us a good chance of actually winning this competition.'

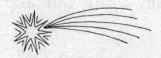

Mildred was still outside the gates. She had taken Star for a walk through the trees, keeping close to the wall so that no one could possibly see them. It really was an ideal task, being the Lantern Monitor, she reflected, as it meant that she could easily get Star out for a walk in the morning *and* evening without being seen, and, if Tabby could just pull himself together, the two pets could stay in her room all day and she could train the little dog to hide under the bed if anyone came in. He seemed ultra-trainable and anxious to please and was already very steady on the broomstick. Perhaps she could even teach him a few tricks.

'Come on then, in you hop,' she said, opening the holdall.

Star jumped on to the broom and into the bag, flattening himself down helpfully.

'Good boy,' said Mildred, zipping him in. 'You really *are* my little star.'

CHAPTER FOURTEEN

Miss Hardbroom decided that each class should come up with ideas for the competition and select the best one with the aid of their form mistresses – the chosen act to be handed in to the staffroom. Miss Hardbroom and Miss Cackle would then consider all the suggestions carefully and post the winner on the downstairs noticeboard at the end of the week.

Miss Drill's class was bursting with ideas and Enid's dance troupe was very popular with her classmates, but totally *un*popular with Miss Drill, who knew that it wouldn't get past Miss Hardbroom's disapproving eye. In the end, Form Four voted for Ethel's chanting choir when Miss Drill said that perhaps they could incorporate a *small* amount of tap-dancing at the same time.

'I just *know* they'll choose my idea,' gloated Ethel, passing Mildred in the corridor as they both started out on their nightly round of lantern-lighting. 'The Grand Wizard's mad about choral singing so *that's* a start

and I've got *such* a superb voice – my singing tutor told me that I'm impossible to teach because I'm already at such a high standard – have you got something else in your bag, Mildred? It looks absolutely stuffed.'

'Nope,' said Mildred briskly, hastening away down the shadowy corridor before Ethel could investigate further. 'Better get on, or it'll be dark before we've finished.'

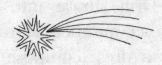

'It's not fair!' yelled Ethel, stomping into the classroom the next morning after breakfast. 'They didn't choose my idea, I can't believe it!'

Form Four were busy gathering up their gym kit, ready to set off for a training session, and everyone looked up surprised.

'How do you know, Ethel?' asked Drusilla.

'I've just seen it on the noticeboard,' snarled Ethel. 'They've chosen Form Five to do a broomstick ballet, called "The Joy of Flying" – huh! What a stupid idea; it's not exactly *original* anyway.'

Despite Ethel's endless sneeriness towards her, Mildred couldn't help feeling quite sorry for Ethel. It was so terribly important to her, being first and best at all costs, and Mildred could see how upset she was not to have the chance to win such an important competition.

Miss Drill strode into the classroom, wearing yet another vibrant outfit. This one was a dress composed of green-lace cobwebs, with a short black and green striped jacket, purple starry stockings and

pointed cowboy boots. 'What's the matter, Ethel?' she asked sternly. 'I could hear your voice halfway down the corridor.'

'I'm sorry, Miss Drill,' said Ethel, trying to sound humble. 'I was just disappointed that our class hasn't been chosen.'

'We're *all* disappointed, Ethel,' said Miss Drill reprovingly. 'Aren't we, girls? But you mustn't be a bad loser, Ethel – everyone knows that losing graciously is just as important as winning in *any* competition! There *are* some excellent dancers in Form Five – and that particular class also has some of the best fliers – yes, Ethel, I *know* you are one of the best in *this* class but it's been decided, and you'll just have to accept that Form Five simply came up with the best idea of all.

'Now then, girls, gather up your kit and hurry down to the cloakroom to change and you can do a spot of broomstick gymnastics to take your minds off your little disappointment. Think of it *this* way, girls: at least you can get on with your usual studies and tasks while Form Five does all the hard work, then all you have to do is cheer them on with the rest of the school and hope they win! Sounds rather *good* news if you ask *me*!'

CHAPTER FIFTEEN

It sounded *brilliant* news to Mildred, who was now free to concentrate on her routine of lantern-lighting and dousing, plus sneaking Star in and out, and working extra hard at her lessons so that she didn't draw any attention to herself. Everything was going so smoothly that she began to wonder if the wishing star had also been a *lucky* star, making things start to go right all the time – even Tabby had calmed down gradually as the days passed. It wasn't long before he realized that Star was no threat at all and one day, when Mildred came up to her room after lessons, she found them both asleep in the holdall under her bed.

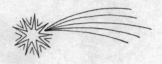

The playground was often so misty first thing that you couldn't see the gates until you were a few feet away, which made the early dog-walk much easier. One morning when the mist was so thick that it provided perfect cover, Mildred took Star a little further into the pine forest and started to teach him a few tricks on the broomstick. He was a natural: unafraid, trusting and desperate to please his rescuer, and Mildred found that he would – and could – do anything she asked.

'Wow,' thought Mildred as she slalomed in and out of the trees with Star leaning into the corners like a pillion rider on a motorbike. 'If only we could have dogs on our brooms, I'd be the school champion!

Even the best cats can't do anything much except sit there!'

Every time it was misty, which was most mornings at that time of year, Mildred taught Star some more tricks. He also came up with a few himself, such as standing on his head and doing a back-flip in mid-air that took him above the broom and over the side, with Mildred zooming underneath to catch him.

Mildred invented a new trick where Star did the usual back-flip with Mildred zooming underneath him. However, this time they started thirty feet up and did several back-flip catches, descending very fast, so that it looked quite graceful, like a tumbling waterfall. Mildred had never had so much fun on a broomstick before.

After a few weeks of morning Star-training, Mildred became so enthusiastic that she began helping him to practise some of the more complicated routines in her room. At first she was a little worried that Tabby would be jealous, but he didn't mind at all. He absolutely hated broomstick flying and couldn't care less about Mildred training anyone else, as long as he still had his place on her pillow at night and lots of cuddles when she was sitting in bed reading.

Star tactfully slept at the end of the bed on Mildred's feet or curled into the back of her knees and Tabby often sneaked under the covers into Mildred's arms, so that she sometimes woke up almost wearing the two of them. On cold nights, Mildred slept

better than she had ever done, wrapped in
her pets like a furry dressing gown. She had
even got used to the clunking bat flap, just
as Maud had said she would.

Mildred hardly saw Maud and Enid at
all during the first few weeks. They often
called for her, but she was usually off
lantern-lighting in the evening when they
all had a spare moment, and by the time
she was back from dousing the candles in
the morning they only had a few minutes
for a quick hello before they all dashed off
to breakfast.

One morning Mildred had just zipped Star into the holdall when there was a knock at the door. 'Who is it?' asked Mildred nervously.

The door burst open and there stood Maud and Enid, dressed and ready for the day, holding their broomsticks. 'Surprise!' said Maud. 'We're coming with you to help, so we can all have half an hour together.'

'Gosh, Mil,' said Enid, who was holding a large jug and a pair of kitchen scissors. 'How on earth do you do this every morning and stay so cheerful?'

'I've sort of got used to it,' said Mildred, glancing at the bag. 'Look, don't worry about me, I'll just nip round on my own. I'll be back in a tick and we can catch up over breakfast.'

'Don't you like us any more, Mil?' asked Maud, sounding really hurt. 'You never ask us into your room these days. Have we *done* something to upset you?'

'Maud's right,' said Enid. 'It feels as if you're avoiding both of us. We haven't had a proper conversation with you since the first day of term.'

Mildred looked desperately at her two friends, longing to tell them but knowing that they would be horrified. She had been having such fun with Star and it had all been so easy, taking him out on lantern duty and hiding him under the bed. She thought of his sweet scruffy face gazing at her and his warmth during the long freezing nights and didn't want to risk losing him.

'Don't be daft!' said Mildred. 'Of *course* I'm not avoiding either of you – I've just been busy, but I really *will* be quicker on my own and –'

'Well, we're coming with you, whether you like it or not,' said Maud. 'Enid's got to get some foliage for her duty as Flower Monitor, haven't you, Enid?'

'That's right,' said Enid. 'So let's go.'

Mildred trailed miserably down the corridors, expertly flipping open the lantern flaps and putting out the candles, followed along by her broomstick and her two friends, and soon they had reached the school gates.

'You really *are* good at this, Millie,' said Maud as Mildred hovered expertly up and over the gateposts, deftly extinguishing the last two lanterns on the way.

They all hovered down and landed on the grass. Mildred led everyone out of sight along the outside of the wall and into the edge of the forest.

'Gosh, Mildred,' said Enid. 'What on *earth* have you got in the bag?'

Star, who was looking forward to his morning runabout and broomstick fun, was wagging his tail and bustling, making the bag and broomstick jerk about madly.

Maud and Enid stared at the bag in amazement.

'This is going to surprise you both,' said Mildred. 'But it really *isn't* as bad as it looks.'

She unzipped the holdall and Star leapt out like a Jack-in-the-box. He was delighted to meet Mildred's friends, jumping up to lick their faces, then setting off in mad circles through the trees, overjoyed to be out after his long night in Mildred's room. Maud and Enid stood with their mouths open, stunned.

'So *this* is why you've been avoiding us!' gasped Maud. 'Oh, Mildred! Miss Hardbroom will go *insane* if she finds out – and you've been doing so well this term. What on earth possessed you? Where did you get him from?'

'I didn't get him from anywhere,' said Mildred, resting on the back of her hovering broom. 'He got *me*! Anyway, it's your fault, Maudie, *you* told me to wish on that shooting star and I wished for a dog – and there he was the next day outside the gates. I couldn't send back a wish-come-true, could I? It wouldn't be right. And he's so clever; he can do hundreds of tricks! Look, I'll show you.'

She called him over and patted the back of the broom.

'Oh, come on, you two,' said Mildred. 'Stop being so grumpy! Just sit there on your brooms and I'll show you all the things he can do. You'll soon see why I had to keep him.'

CHAPTER SIXTEEN

The three friends made their way back through the silent morning corridors with Star zipped neatly into his holdall and Enid carrying the jug, now full of pine-cone branches and jolly twigs with red berries to brighten up their grey-stone classroom.

They hurried into Mildred's room and closed the door behind them. Mildred opened the holdall and Star immediately leapt out and dived under the bed.

'I don't know what Einstein's going to say when he wakes up in the spring!' laughed Mildred. 'Well then, what did you think of him?'

'He's incredible, Mildred,' said Maud, 'and *you're* incredible *with* him. I've never seen you fly like that.'

'He's like part of you,' said Enid. 'Like another arm or leg. I can see why you're crazy about him – not that it makes things any easier. H.B. will still go mad when she finds out.'

'*If* she finds out,' said Mildred, 'and *we* aren't telling anyone, are we?'

'Of *course* not,' said Maud. 'Anyway, you've done brilliantly so far – even your best friends didn't suspect a thing, so maybe you'll be able to hide him till the end of term. *Tell* you what, let's all go and watch

Form Five rehearsing for their broomstick ballet at lunchtime. They're doing the first dress rehearsal in the Great Hall; it's supposed to be fantastic.'

'That would be *so* nice,' said Mildred, feeling a wave of relief that her two best friends were in on her secret. 'It'll be great if we win, especially as Form Five are doing all the hard work – at least there's no way I can mess up someone else's broomstick display!'

They all laughed, remembering the now legendary Hallowe'en when they were first-years and Ethel had spitefully lent Mildred a broom with a spell on it, which had wrecked the display. Everything had turned out well in the end, but Mildred still had nightmares about it.

The broomstick ballet *was* fantastic. Miss Hardbroom had taken charge of the project with the help of Miss Bat, who was providing a rousing piano accompaniment, and Miss Mould the art mistress, who had designed some wonderful flowing costumes for the four aerial ballerinas. Each dancer represented different aspects of night flying. There was an owl-dancer in magnificent wings and a head-dress made from hand-sewn fluttering silk feathers, two dancers draped in midnight-blue robes sewn with

star-shaped sequins, and the principal
dancer, who was bedecked in silver and blue
to represent moonlight. The dancers were
set against a beautiful deep-blue backdrop,
with a huge white moon and stars picked out
in luminous paint which glowed magically
under the candelabras. Every class had
worked tirelessly, painting the backdrop
and sewing on sequins and feathers, so
that the whole school felt involved in their

competition entry.

Mildred, Enid and Maud sat in the front row with a crowd of excited spectators and watched as Form Five performed the first showing of an act which really did express 'the joy of flying'.

'I think we could actually win with that!' enthused Maud as they hurried to grab some food before lunch-break was over. 'It was really beautiful.'

'No it wasn't,' said Ethel, who had come up behind them without anyone noticing. 'Just run-of-the-mill, if you ask me.'

'No one *is* asking you, Ethel,' said Mildred. 'Anyway, you aren't a judge, thank goodness, so we'll just have to keep our fingers crossed and leave it up to them. Don't you *want* us to win the swimming pool?'

'You think you're really great now, don't you, Mildred Hubble?' said Ethel, her voice rising dangerously. 'Just because you've lit a few lanterns without burning the school down, you think everyone's suddenly dying to hear what *you* think about everything.'

'No I don't, Ethel,' said Mildred wearily, 'and I'm not getting into an argument about nothing, so why don't you find someone else to pick on?'

Ethel stalked away down the corridor and Mildred felt a sudden stab of alarm as she imagined what Ethel would do if she found out about Star.

CHAPTER SEVENTEEN

The competition was to take place at the Supreme Magician's residence – a vast, rambling castle with a hundred and fifty rooms, one of which was a gigantic hall, large enough for three schools to fit in at once, cheering on their acts in front of the three judges. There were thirty schools for sorcery, magic and witchcraft scattered about the country, most of them flying in from isolated places, and it would take ten days for all thirty acts to be judged at a rate of three a day, five days a week. Miss Cackle's Academy was to perform on the last day of the competition along with Pentangle's and Moonridge High.

By a fantastic stroke of luck, Miss Cackle's Academy was only three mountains away from the Supreme Magician's castle, which meant that they would not have to stay overnight. Mildred had been racking her brains for a furtive way of bringing Star with her under the watchful eye of Miss Drill (who was, unfortunately, proving every bit as vigilant as Miss Hardbroom, despite the zany outfits), and Mildred breathed a sigh of relief that she would only be gone for the daytime hours – when Star was used to having his long sleep under her bed anyway.

Miss Cackle and Miss Hardbroom sat in the staffroom with all the teachers on the night before their schools' auditions.

'I think that's everything covered, Miss Cackle,' said Miss Hardbroom, who had just read out their travel plans in minute detail, including the transport of costumes and scenery, plus the making of nearly two hundred packed lunches.

'Do you think we might actually win?' asked Miss Drill. 'I've seen one of the rehearsals and I must say it did look quite *special*.'

'I think we have an excellent chance,' replied Miss Hardbroom. 'My only worry is whether there might have been an *over-abundance* of broomstick ballets during the previous nine days. If so, the judges might

be a little bored by yet another ballet routine. I must say, I rather wish we weren't the very last act of all.'

'Oh, I don't know, Miss Hardbroom,' said Miss Cackle. 'Surely it's worse to be at the beginning, nearly two weeks earlier! The judges are much more likely to remember the last act than the first one!'

'And the judges *are* all getting on for a hundred years old,' laughed Miss Mould. 'So it's better to be fresh in their memories, I'd say!'

'Now, now, Miss Mould!' scolded Miss Cackle, a twinkle in her eye. 'We're *none* of us getting any younger and I'm sure that the combined brains of the three most honoured sorcerers in the country are quite adequate to judge a talent competition!'

'Well, if you don't mind,' announced Miss Hardbroom, 'I'm off to bed, as there will be a great deal to contend with tomorrow morning. One last thing, Miss Mould, could you assist me with taking the costumes down to the front hall, ready for Form Five to tie on to their broomsticks in the morning? I shall be carrying the rolled-up backdrop underneath my own broom for the journey, as it really *is* rather unwieldy and we don't want any accidents before we get there! All pupils to be assembled in the playground by ten o'clock sharp, ready for take-off. Well, goodnight, everyone.'

'Goodnight, Miss Hardbroom,' called Miss Cackle as Miss Hardbroom swept out of the door. She was going to say 'pleasant dreams', but somehow she couldn't imagine her deputy dreaming of anything but school rules and timetables, so there didn't seem much point.

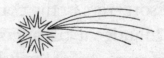

The following morning Mildred was up and dressed even earlier than usual, ready to zoom round the corridors, take Star for his walk and hurry back to hide him under the bed before the journey. She put down a bowl of catfood for Tabby, left the door ajar so he could go for his morning wander, stuffed Star into the holdall and set off down the corridor.

She was now an expert Lantern Monitor, taking her duties extremely seriously. She had changed all the candles the day before and polished the glass so that there was no maintenance to do that morning and she was making very good time. She soon reached the entrance hall and flew up to douse the candle in the large lantern which hung above the main doors leading to the playground.

It was a cheerful, sunny morning, most unusual for the academy. Mildred glanced around at the rays slanting in through the windows and noticed the rail with the four ballet costumes, awaiting broom-transport. Star was already wriggling about in the bag, keen to have his breakfast on the grass and a run about through the trees.

'Stop it!' giggled Mildred. 'You'll have me off the broom!'

'Talking to yourself now, are you, Mildred Hubble?' said a sharp voice right behind her.

Mildred jumped and almost overbalanced as she was now fifteen feet up and not expecting anyone to be there.

'Ethel!' she exclaimed. 'Careful! You made me jump – what are you doing here?'

'Following *you*,' said Ethel unpleasantly, hovering next to Mildred and nudging the holdall with her foot. 'You weren't *quite* quick enough outside the gates yesterday. I was looking out of the window when the mist cleared, just in time to see you putting something in your bag. What was it, Mildred? A badger? A large hedgehog? It was definitely an animal, that's for sure.'

'It was only Tabby,' said Mildred, feeling desperate, as the holdall was now noticeably beginning to judder. 'He's in there now, so I'd better get on, Ethel, if you don't mind,

or we'll *both* be late for take-off.'

Unfortunately, just at that moment Tabby (unmistakeable as he was the only tabby cat in the school) strolled underneath them and out into the yard through the communal cat flap set into the wall.

'I think *not*,' said Ethel. 'So, what *have* you got in the bag, Mildred? Come on, show me!'

Mildred had flipped open the lantern door and was poised with the candle-snuffer when Ethel made a dive for the zip on the holdall.

CHAPTER EIGHTEEN

Everything happened at once. Ethel yanked the zip open and Star's head sprang into view, barking. Ethel was thrown off balance and seized Mildred, who also overbalanced. Mildred tried to stop them all from falling by grabbing the lantern but, to her horror, she only succeeded in wrenching it clean out of the wall. They watched helplessly as it hurtled across the slate floor below, smashing open and setting light to the costumes.

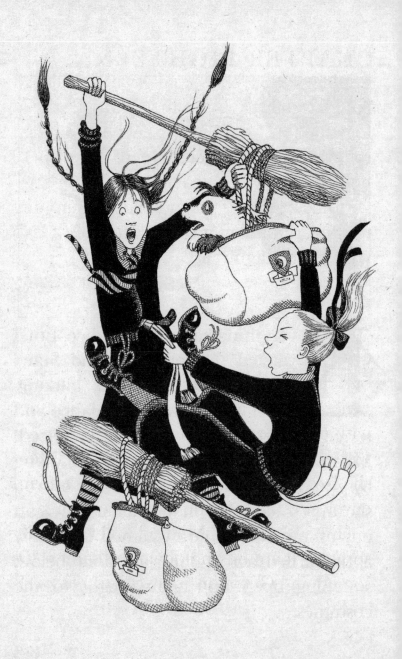

Dangling from both brooms, Ethel gripping Mildred's holdall and Mildred hanging on to Star, they twirled down together like a helicopter with a broken rotor, fortunately cushioned by Ethel's holdall as they hit the flagstones.

'Quick, Ethel!' yelled Mildred, jumping up and rummaging in her holdall. 'Grab your fire extinguisher!'

Star was bouncing up and down barking hysterically, but the only thing Mildred could think of was putting out the fire. She found her own fire extinguisher, stood back and aimed it at the base of the flames, which were roaring up all four costumes with heart-stopping speed. Ethel lay frozen with shock on top of the holdall where she had fallen, watching as clouds of foam enveloped the burning mass of clothing.

'Ethel!' bellowed Mildred, still frantically spraying foam up and down the flames. '*Do* something! Get your fire extinguisher *now*!'

Ethel snapped out of her trance. She

scrambled to her feet, pulled her fire extinguisher out of the bag and aimed it at the remaining shreds of the costumes until the flames were completely engulfed.

The hallway was now a blackened mess, knee-deep in foam, with bits of charred material floating delicately through the air. Mildred aimed one last burst of foam into the broken lantern.

'It's **OK**, Ethel,' she said, 'it's out.'

Star had stopped barking and had tucked himself behind Mildred's legs, looking shamefaced. Something was clearly wrong and he was rather worried that it might be his fault. Mildred and Ethel stood staring at each other in a state of shock. They were both covered in soot, their clothes drenched, the ballet costumes utterly ruined.

'We are going to be in *such* trouble,' murmured Mildred, glancing nervously towards the door.

'You certainly *are*, Mildred Hubble,' said Miss Hardbroom's unwelcome voice as she materialized silently from a dark alcove. 'This is quite unbelievable! You *do* realize that we now have absolutely *no* prospect of even *entering* the competition, let alone winning it – added to which, the two of you have almost burnt down the school.'

'It was an accident, Miss Hardbroom,' said Ethel, beginning to sob. 'Mildred had a dog in her bag and I was investigating.'

'It wasn't *my* fault!' protested Mildred.

'I was on my morning lantern round, minding my own business, when Ethel flew up behind me and grabbed my bag and –'

'I didn't just grab it,' said Ethel. 'I was trying to stop you from hiding that dog!'

Miss Hardbroom brushed a floating piece of charred owl costume from her nose as they all looked down at Star, now cowering behind Mildred.

'Go to Miss Cackle's office,' said Miss Hardbroom in a voice quivering with anger, 'and wait for me there while I attend to this mess. Then we will need to gather everyone together in the Great Hall, where you can both explain to your fellow pupils why all their hard work has been in vain. *I'll* take the dog, Mildred,' she added as the two girls turned to leave the scene of their crime, followed closely by Star.

'He needs to go out, Miss Hardbroom,' gibbered Mildred. 'Could I just –'

'No, you couldn't,' snapped Miss Hardbroom. '*I'll* take him if he needs to go out, Mildred, he's no longer any concern of yours. Give me your sash so that I can use it as a lead.'

Mildred took off her sash and knelt down to tie it round Star's neck. 'Do as you're told, won't you?' she said in a quavering voice, as he tried to jump up and lick her face. 'Be a good dog – he's called Star, Miss Hardbroom.'

She handed the makeshift lead to the terrifying teacher but to Mildred's surprise the little dog didn't struggle at all. He just sat down, stuck his nose in the air and began to howl mournfully, as if he knew that all was lost.

CHAPTER NINETEEN

'Have you heard the news?' gasped Maud, bursting into Enid's room.

'What?' asked Enid. 'What's happened?'

'It's really terrible,' said Maud, 'in every way you can think of! Ethel and Mildred had a fight and knocked over one of the lanterns and all the ballet costumes were burnt to a cinder *and* they nearly burnt the school down *and* Miss Hardbroom's got Star!'

'What about the competition?' asked Enid.

'What *about* the competition?' said Maud grimly. 'There isn't going to *be* a competition, not for our school anyway – not without costumes.'

'Poor Mildred,' said Enid. 'Everyone's going to be so cross with her – the teachers, the dancers, the entire school! It's going to be awful.'

'At least it wasn't *just* her,' said Maud. 'It sounds as if Ethel was at least equally to blame, though I'm sure she'll do her best to wriggle out of it. It's the dog I feel dreadful about. Mildred really loved him and she'd done such brilliant work with him – that flying routine was good enough to go on the stage.'

They suddenly looked at each other as an idea crossed their minds at *exactly* the same time.

Mildred and Ethel waited in Miss Cackle's office in a state of terror, both wondering if they would be expelled. Ethel was just as scared as Mildred and for once couldn't think of a single gibe to hurl in her direction. There really seemed to be no way out of the huge mess they were in.

The door suddenly crashed open and Miss Hardbroom marched in, leading Star on Mildred's sash, followed by a very serious-faced Miss Cackle. Star sprang hopefully towards Mildred and was sharply yanked back by Miss Hardbroom. Both teachers sat on the other side of Miss Cackle's desk facing the wrongdoers, while Star slunk underneath, his eyes fixed longingly on Mildred.

Miss Cackle had just begun to speak when there was a soft tap at the door.

'Who is it?' called Miss Hardbroom irritably.

The door opened very slowly to reveal Maud and Enid looking petrified.

'What is it, Maud?' asked Miss Cackle.

'Um . . . we heard about the costumes –' said Maud.

'– and we thought of a way that we could still enter the competition,' explained Enid.

'That's very school-spirited of you, girls,' said Miss Cackle, 'but I'm afraid it really is too late.'

'But it *isn't*!' burst out Maud. 'The dog is amazing! Mildred does a flying routine with him that's absolutely brilliant – we've seen it, haven't we, Enid? Honestly, Miss Cackle, it's funny and clever –'

'And the dog's so cute,' said Enid, getting carried away. 'And Mildred flies the best we've ever seen her when she's with him – doesn't she, Maud?'

They carried on in this fashion, singing the flying duo's praises, getting more and more enthusiastic, until Miss Hardbroom put up a hand to stop them.

Everyone stared down at Star, who didn't *look* like a competition winner, hunched in the shadows, trying to keep out of the way.

'I don't *think* so, Maud,' said Miss Hardbroom. 'Even if what you say *is* true, we don't have any time to put the pair through their paces and we certainly don't want the academy to be made a laughing stock in front of such an illustrious panel of judges – don't you agree, Miss Cackle?'

Mildred stood up and took a deep breath. '*Please*, Miss Cackle,' she said, trying to keep her voice from trembling. 'I think we *could* do it really. I've been training him for weeks on end and the auditions are only ten minutes long. I know we could manage to keep everyone entertained for at least that long and the school entry *is* called "The Joy of Flying", so we could still enter under that title – *please*, Miss Cackle, it's the only way I can possibly make amends for messing up our chances. Wouldn't it be better than nothing – to *try* and win?'

Incredibly, Miss Cackle was moved by Mildred's plea. She over-rode Miss Hardbroom's protests and announced that she agreed with Mildred – that it *was* better to make an attempt at winning than to give up.

At this point Ethel couldn't restrain herself any longer. 'But it's not fair, Miss Cackle!' she exclaimed. 'It's that stupid dog's fault that we can't do the ballet and I think –'

Miss Hardbroom fixed Ethel with one of her most blood-curdling stares. 'Miss Cackle is speaking!' she said icily.

'Thank you, Miss Hardbroom,' continued Miss Cackle. 'As I was saying, Mildred, I've decided to trust you, *and* the

opinion of your two friends here, mainly because I think I *know* you and I don't think you would risk putting yourself up in front of the school if you didn't feel sure you could do it – am I right?'

'Yes, Miss Cackle,' said Mildred gratefully.

'Well then,' said Miss Cackle, 'you'd better take the dog and get yourselves ready to assemble for take-off at ten o'clock as planned. Miss Hardbroom and I will deliver the news to all the pupils and tell them that we *will* be competing after all.'

'Just a moment,' said Miss Hardbroom to Ethel, who was attempting to sneak out with the others. 'Would you just stay behind – I have a few questions I'd like to ask you . . .'

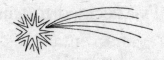

As soon as they were out of range of Miss Cackle's study, the three friends hurled their arms round each other and jumped about.

'Thank you so much for saving me,' said Mildred to Maud and Enid, scooping up Star who was ecstatic to be back in her arms.

'You're not out of the woods yet,' said Maud. 'You've got to actually *win* the competition and Pentangle's have probably got something brilliant up their sleeve – they usually have.'

'And Form Five are going to *hate* you and Ethel,' warned Enid.

'It wasn't really my fault about the costumes,' said Mildred. 'Ethel knew I was hiding Star in the holdall and she grabbed it; that's why we fell. I s'pose I shouldn't have had him in the bag in the first place, but if she hadn't been snooping it would never have happened.'

'Whatever the reason,' said Maud, 'it's a bit hard on Form Five after all their hard work. Even if you do win, they're still not going to be pleased.'

CHAPTER TWENTY

They *weren't* pleased. All four broomstick-ballet dancers were in tears when everyone lined up in the playground with their broomsticks, cats and packed lunches, and Mildred felt terrible that she had been part-responsible for ending their dream, even though it really hadn't been her fault.

Before departure, Miss Cackle addressed everyone as they stood lined up in rows.

'We still have a small chance of winning this competition, girls,' she announced. 'Mildred Hubble and Ethel Hallow would like to offer their sincere apologies for the unfortunate accident which ruined the costumes. However, I would like everyone to find it in their hearts to cheer on Mildred and her stray dog, who are to be a last-minute replacement, which I am assured is very much worth the judges' consideration. Onward and upward, girls! We must all

hope for the best!'

It should have been such a happy occasion: a flight out from school for the day, with the girls chatting excitedly. The possibility of winning a fantastic prize would normally have sent ripples of joy throughout the school but everyone's spirits had been doused as thoroughly as the flaming costumes and no one spoke as they soared above the treetops, blotting out the sky like a giant flock of starlings.

143

Mildred was having quite a hard time, as both Tabby and Star were travelling on her broom. There was not enough room for both of them and Tabby had climbed on to her shoulder, while Star was sitting upright, surefooted and calm, delighted to be back with his dearest owner. Every now and then he couldn't restrain himself from giving a joyful bark, which brought a disapproving glance from Miss Hardbroom.

Mildred knew that all eyes were watching her and Star curiously, knowing that they were the school's only chance of winning the competition and wondering if they were really any good. She longed to zoom off and do a loop-the-loop to show her fellow pupils what they could do, but everyone would just have to wait.

The party stopped in a clearing for their packed lunches and Mildred bravely made her way over to Form Five and the four thwarted ballet dancers, who looked up sullenly from their cheese sandwiches, silently daring her to speak. The other members of Form Five, though busy with their own lunchboxes, were obviously all ears.

'I just wanted to say I'm *so* sorry,' Mildred plunged in. 'I thought the ballet was fantastic – I even sewed some of the owl feathers and *I* was looking forward to it as much as the whole school was. I really *didn't* do it on purpose; it was a terrible accident. I suppose I'm asking you to forgive me and to wish Star and me the best – it would mean the world if you could – but I'll understand if you just hate me.'

For a moment no one spoke, then Edna, the principal dancer, got to her feet. All the other members of the school, including the teachers, were sitting down and usually Miss Hardbroom would have called for the two girls to do the same but this time no one said a word as all eyes turned to Mildred and Edna, wondering what would happen.

Edna held out her hand to Mildred.

'Forgiven,' she said. 'I can't say I'm *thrilled* about it, but at least we'll still have a chance to win the swimming pool. Just try not to mess it up this time, OK? Of course we'll be rooting for you. Come on, everyone –' she turned to face the assembled mass of teachers and pupils – 'let's all wish the best of luck to Mildred and her dog. *I* certainly will.'

The whole school, taking their lead from Edna's amazing generosity, jumped to their feet shouting 'Good luck!' and 'You can do it!' while Enid and Maud even threw their hats in the air, which was perhaps overdoing it a bit in the circumstances. Tears of relief sprang into Mildred's eyes as she watched the storm cloud of anger dissolve like the morning mist, leaving everyone chatting normally.

Miss Cackle smiled good-naturedly at her flock. 'Edna has such terrific team spirit,' she said, taking a sip of tea from her flask. 'Wouldn't you agree, Miss Hardbroom? I can't think of many girls who would show such forbearance in a situation like this – except perhaps Mildred herself.'

'She hasn't *won* yet, Miss Cackle,' said Miss Hardbroom tartly, 'and we don't even know if this dog can do anything more than just sit on a broom – and steal sandwiches!' she added as Star stealthily extracted an egg sandwich from Mildred's lunchbox when he thought no one was looking.

'We can only hope, Miss Hardbroom,' said Miss Cackle, 'so let us all fervently hope that he *is* as special as Mildred says.'

CHAPTER TWENTY-ONE

The Supreme Magician's castle was bustling with activity as they swooped down to land in the central courtyard (a little shakily for the first-years, who hadn't been flying long). Once they had got their breath back they were escorted to the Great Hall, which was three times the size of the Great Hall at Miss Cackle's Academy. It was already two-thirds full with the pupils of Pentangle's, resplendent in their purple uniforms, and the trainee wizards of Moonridge High, dressed in dark grey suits and black ties with a single crescent moon in the centre. At the front of the audience stood a raised platform with three throne-like chairs padded in green velvet. Facing the audience was a magnificent stage complete with gold curtains, which were closed ready for the opening act.

'Who's on first?' asked Mildred, her confidence draining away, as she contemplated the expectant audience and the enormous stage.

'I think it's Moonridge High,' replied Maud, consulting the piece of paper that she had found on her chair. 'They're doing a "Battle of the Broomsticks", whatever that is, and then it's Pentangle's. Oh, look, they're doing a broomstick ballet just like ours. We're on last with "The Joy of Flying" so you'll be a nice surprise for the judges.'

'Let's hope it *is* a nice surprise!' laughed Enid. 'I s'pose it helps that we would have been doing another ballet after Pentangle's, so you and Star will at least be different.'

'Shh,' said Maud. 'Here come the judges.'

Everyone leapt to their feet as the judges passed through the crowd on their way to their thrones, turning to greet the audience as they stepped up on to the platform.

The Supreme Magician and the Chief Wizard had traditional long flowing beards, and the Magician's robe was covered in embroidered stars while the Chief Wizard's was plain dark purple. Both wore gowns like university professors over their robes, and the Grand High Witch was dressed in plain black, with ankle-length white hair spread dramatically over her shoulders like a cloak. Despite her severe style of clothing, the Grand High Witch had a kindly look about her face with deep crow's feet round her eyes as if she laughed a lot.

'Welcome to you all,' said the Chief Wizard, smiling vaguely at everyone. 'First of all, let me thank the Supreme Magician for his generosity in lending us this magnificent

castle for the most exciting competition of
the century! My fellow judges and I have
certainly been thoroughly entertained for
the last two weeks by all your efforts and we
have been most impressed with the standard
so far. Your three schools are the final acts in
a long line of superb entries and I'm sure we
won't be disappointed. So, without further
ado, let us see what Moonridge High has in
store for us!'

The judges turned to face the stage, settling themselves comfortably on their thrones. Everyone fell silent as the curtains drew back to reveal eight Moonridge boys on broomsticks, four of them dressed as wizards, complete with flowing false beards, the other four dressed as dragons. The costumes were excellent and the music (vigorously played on a grand piano in the wings by the Moonridge chanting master) was a stirring rendition of the 'William

Tell Overture' as they zoomed about the stage, the wizards zapping the dragons and the dragons trying to knock the wizards off their broomsticks. There was only one mishap, when a wizard's beard snagged on a dragon's wing and pinged across the stage, but the judges laughed good-humouredly, and the piece drew to a dramatic close with the wizards chasing the dragons out over the audience's heads, before landing back on stage to take their bows.

The audience erupted from their seats, cheering and clapping, especially the Moonridge supporters. Mildred's stomach lurched even deeper into her boots as she imagined herself up there on her own, relying on Star to get it right in front of all these people.

'How do I get myself into situations like this every single time?' she whispered to Maud. 'I was really looking forward to our ballet and suddenly it's all up to me! The Moonridge boys were good, weren't they?'

'Not as good as you'll be,' said Maud loyally. 'Just take some deep breaths – you're going to be fine.'

Tabby was snuggled on Mildred's lap. All the cats were sitting with their owners; everywhere you looked there were black cats – on laps, on shoulders and draped along the backs of chairs. Only Mildred had a tabby, showing up like a striped apron against her black gymslip, and of course Star, who was curled round her ankles so

she couldn't go anywhere without him.

While Pentangle's were performing their ballet, Miss Drill, who was dressed in a rather sensible dark blue suit (Miss Hardbroom had asked her to tone it down a bit for the trip), tapped Mildred on the shoulder. 'You're on next, Mildred,' she whispered. 'You'd better bring the dog and come backstage, ready for lift-off – so to speak!'

Mildred got up and beckoned for Star to follow her. 'Could you hang on to Tab for me?' she asked Maud, plonking the little cat on to her friend's lap. 'They won't both fit on the broom.'

'Course,' said Maud. 'Best of luck, Millie.'

'Fingers and toes crossed!' whispered Enid. 'Just pretend you're out in the forest, flying for fun!'

'Shh!' said someone from Pentangle's in the row behind. 'We're trying to watch the ballet!'

'Sorry,' said Mildred, crouching down as she shuffled out of the row of seats, some of the cats arching their backs and spitting at the sight of the jaunty little dog with his waving tail.

CHAPTER TWENTY-TWO

Mildred crept along behind Miss Drill, who led her out of the hall, round to a large dressing room directly behind the stage. It was full of props and costumes, including Moonridge's wizard and dragon costumes, now neatly stacked in a corner. Mildred could hear the 'Ride of the Valkyries' thundering impressively out of the grand piano as Pentangle's performers twirled and plummeted around the stage, presenting their 'Hallowe'en' broomstick ballet in gorgeous flowing silk robes. There

was a stone archway at each end of the wall and Mildred peeked through in awe as the dancers zipped expertly past.

Miss Hardbroom was unrolling the moon and stars backdrop, which had fortunately been stored in Miss Cackle's study and escaped the blaze.

'Ah, Mildred,' said Miss Hardbroom, beckoning her. 'Come and help me with this, it's a trifle heavy.'

Mildred rushed to help, joined eagerly by Star who grabbed the edge with his teeth, taking backward jumps, growling gleefully.

'Just the two of us, Mildred!' said Miss Hardbroom. 'We don't need canine assistance, thank you!'

'Drop it!' said Mildred firmly.

Star immediately let go of the backdrop, scampered round the back of Mildred's ankles and sat gazing up at her, awaiting further command.

'Impressive, Mildred!' said Miss Drill admiringly. 'He certainly does what you tell him. Now then, here's your broomstick – do you need anything else, piano music from Miss Bat perhaps? She is most willing to play any music you like, if that will help.'

'I think I'd rather do our act without it,' said Mildred, 'if that's OK. I've never rehearsed with Miss Bat and it might not work if I'm trying to fit the moves to music that I don't know.'

Miss Hardbroom sat back on her heels, smoothing the last few feet of unrolled backdrop. 'What *are* you going to do out there, Mildred?' she asked searchingly. 'I must say, this does seem to be a huge gamble, sending the Worst Witch and a completely untested dog out in front of an audience of hundreds, in the vain hope that everything will go right – which is usually the opposite in your case, from what I remember.'

'I'll do my best, Miss Hardbroom,' mumbled Mildred, trying to ignore the hurtful dig about being the Worst Witch.

The music came to a halt with a flourish

and once again they heard the audience burst from their seats, clapping and cheering, sounding to Mildred's ears, as if they must have been the best performers of all.

Miss Drill noticed the crushed expression on Mildred's face and dropped a kindly arm round her shoulders. 'Come on, Mildred,' she said encouragingly. 'You know, it's very brave of you to take this on all by yourself. I'm sure you can do it – you and your little friend here.'

The curtains closed and Pentangle's ballet team streamed through the archways into the dressing room, laughing noisily and trailing their brooms along behind them.

Miss Hardbroom and Mildred, assisted by Miss Drill (who had to be careful on account of her bad knee), dragged the backdrop through one of the arches and hung it up on the back wall of the stage. It looked very small, like a painting above a fireplace, rather than a piece of scenery.

'It's a bit small, isn't it?' commented Miss

Drill. 'I think Miss Mould must have got the measurements wrong.'

The size of the backdrop was the least of Mildred's worries as she stared around the gigantic stage, her heart banging so loudly she felt sure that everyone must be able to hear it. Star could tell that his adored mistress was anxious, so he shuffled up next to her, wagging the tip of his tail just to let her know that he was there. Mildred smoothed his head with one hand and held the broomstick with the other, wondering if she could possibly back out.

'You can't back out now, Mildred,' said Miss Hardbroom, appearing to read her mind. 'For some unknown reason, Miss Cackle is convinced that you and this creature can make us proud –'

'And I'm sure she *will*, Miss Hardbroom!' interjected Miss Drill, smiling encouragingly at Mildred, who had turned very pale and looked as though she was going to be sick.

'Come along, Miss Drill,' said Miss

Hardbroom crisply. 'We'd better be off – time for the dancing duo to show what they're made of!'

Miss Drill lagged behind for a moment as Miss Hardbroom strode through the archway into the dressing room. 'You'll be fine, Mildred,' she said soothingly. 'Just be yourself!' Then she hurried after Miss Hardbroom, leaving Mildred feeling as tiny as an ant, alone in the centre of the stage.

CHAPTER TWENTY-THREE

Suddenly Mildred heard the Chief Wizard on the other side of the curtain. 'And now,' he was announcing with great enthusiasm, 'the last entry in the competition: a surprise act from Miss Cackle's Academy entitled "The Joy of Flying".'

Mildred snapped out of her terrified trance and commanded her broomstick to hover. 'Up you jump, Star,' she said, remembering Enid's advice about pretending to be in the forest. 'We're going to have some fun.'

And they did!

The training sessions had paid off – and Star was thrilled that he was out of trouble, making him even happier than usual to do all the things he loved for the mistress he adored. He leapt from the broom in mid-air, while Mildred set off in a perfect nosedive to catch him. He jumped from the back of the stick over Mildred's head into her lap, then back again the other way. He stood on his head, and together they zoomed out over the audience and buzzed Enid and Maud to shrieks of delight, then flew several loop-the-loops – Star jumping on top of the broom each time it rolled so that he didn't fall off. The finale was 'The Waterfall', starting right up near the ceiling and tumbling down almost forty feet, before landing the right way up at the front of the stage, facing the judges.

Star leapt into Mildred's arms and she bowed low, laughing with relief as the audience sprang to their feet, cheering, stamping, even whistling their appreciation.

Mildred could hear Maud and Enid's voices above the cacophony. She searched the crowd and saw Miss Cackle's friendly face wreathed in smiles. Even Miss Hardbroom looked pleased, in an exasperated kind of way, and Miss Drill was waving her arms dementedly in the air, cheering at the top of her voice.

The most amazing part of all was the judges' reaction. They all solemnly got to their feet, and Mildred thought for an alarming moment that they were going to walk out; instead they held their arms out towards Mildred and clapped the loudest of all. Star decided to join in and began barking joyfully. It was the best day of Mildred's whole life.

The Supreme Magician turned and gestured to the audience to quieten down. Mildred hastily seized Star by the nose as he was having such a wonderful doggy barking session that he couldn't stop. 'That's enough,' whispered Mildred.

'Well,' said the Supreme Magician, 'that was certainly a surprise act, my dear. A little un*usual* – a dog on a broomstick – are they allowed, your Grand Highness?' he asked, turning to the Grand High Witch.

'There isn't actually *any* rule concerning which sort of animal is allowed on a broom,' said the Grand High Witch. 'It could be anything at all, even an elephant, except for its size! It's just become a tradition that most schools have cats because they are small and easy to care for – and there's nothing in any rule-book stating that they have to be black cats. It's just turned out that way over the years because black ones are less conspicuous for night flying.'

Mildred was thrilled to hear this. Perhaps

Tabby wasn't such a misfit after all.

'We were looking for Star Quality,' continued the Supreme Magician.

'Which these two have in vast quantities,' affirmed the Chief Wizard.

'I think we have our winner,' said the Grand High Witch. 'Are we all agreed?'

'Agreed!' said the Chief Wizard.

'Agreed!' said the Grand High Witch.

'Agreed!' said the Supreme Magician. 'And the winner of the Swimming-Pool Competition is Miss Cackle's Academy with "The Joy of Flying"!'

CHAPTER TWENTY-FOUR

The flight home was so different to the miserable outward journey. The whole school was buzzing with happiness and Mildred thought she might actually explode with joy. The teachers had given up trying to calm the pupils down, especially as everyone kept begging Mildred to do some more tricks with Star and she couldn't resist a few loop-the-loops when Miss Hardbroom's back was turned.

When they arrived back at the academy Mildred escaped to her room with Maud and Enid, but she was soon besieged by pupils from all over the school pleading for an audience with Star, who was delighted to oblige, giving a paw and bouncing around the room.

Mildred picked up Tabby and gave him his favourite upside-down cuddle, so that

he wouldn't feel left out, but he was worried by the crowd and soon wriggled out of Mildred's arms, taking cover by leaping on top of the wardrobe.

Mildred began to enjoy herself. Everyone kept thanking her for winning the competition and asking if Star could

do some tricks, so Mildred made the broomstick hover, and Star impressed them all by standing on his head. The room was already crammed to bursting with admirers when there was a knock at the door.

'*Another* fan!' laughed Maud, sweeping the door open.

'I'm not sure you could actually call me a "fan", Maud,' said Miss Hardbroom, who was standing outside in her usual disapproving manner.

Everyone froze, including Star, who was still standing on his head on the back of Mildred's broom.

'Miss Cackle wants to see you in her office, Mildred,' announced Miss Hardbroom, 'and you'd better bring the dog – preferably on all four legs.'

'Yes, Miss Hardbroom,' said Mildred, clicking her fingers at Star, who did a perfect back-flip from the broom, landing at her feet. The back-flip somehow looked slightly cheeky with Miss Hardbroom watching sternly from the doorway.

Mildred gave a last, anxious glance back at the room full of silent pupils, Maud and Enid holding up crossed fingers and mouthing 'good luck'.

Mildred followed Miss Hardbroom through the winding corridors, past the unlit lanterns, which she now thought of as 'her' lanterns after weeks of lighting them so diligently each night. She wondered sadly who would be lighting them now, as it seemed unlikely she would still be allowed after the costumes fiasco.

'Where did the dog actually *come* from Mildred?' asked Miss Hardbroom.

Star was now slinking behind his mistress, trying to keep as far away from Miss Hardbroom as possible.

'I'm not sure you'll believe me, Miss Hardbroom,' explained Mildred, 'but I saw a shooting star fall behind the school gates – ages ago on the first day of term – and I

wished for a dog and the next morning I found Star outside the school gates! I know you'll probably think I'm being silly –'

'I *don't* actually, Mildred,' said Miss Hardbroom. 'I feel I should tell you that *I* saw the same shooting star and wished that we would win the swimming-pool competition. The likelihood of two wishes on the same star coming true would seem, to me, to be *very* remote, yet they *did*. Interesting, isn't it?'

CHAPTER TWENTY-FIVE

Miss Cackle was seated behind her desk when Mildred and Miss Hardbroom entered her study.

'Ah, Mildred, my dear!' she said in her most friendly voice. Mildred's spirits rose – being called 'my dear' was a very good sign. 'Congratulations to our winning team,' continued Miss Cackle. 'Sit down.'

'Sit!' said Mildred to Star.

'No dear!' laughed Miss Cackle. 'I meant *you*.'

Mildred sat down shyly and Star crept

under her chair and flattened himself into the floor, remembering the last time he had been in the room.

'Miss Hardbroom and I have been discussing your superb performance at the Supreme Magician's castle today,' said Miss Cackle, 'and we both agreed that you flew like a different person.'

'And we could not help noticing,' continued Miss Hardbroom, 'that you seemed to be completely in tune with your new dog-companion here – a truly magnificent performance, in fact.'

'Thank you, Miss Hardbroom,' said Mildred, 'he's just so good at flying. He always was, right from the first time I put him on the broom. I'm only the pilot really, steering him round so he can show off all his tricks.'

'That's rather *over*-modest, Mildred,' said Miss Cackle 'There was a lot of input from you, especially in such difficult manoeuvres as the loop-the-loop –'

'And nosedives, Mildred!' interrupted Miss Hardbroom. 'I seem to remember you had a great deal of trouble with your nosedives at the beginning of your school career.'

At this point, Mildred hunched her shoulders nervously up round her ears, unsure of what the two teachers were actually trying to tell her. They were managing to sound admiring and disapproving at the same time and she wasn't quite sure what was coming next.

'Don't look so worried, Mildred,' said Miss Cackle, nodding at her encouragingly. 'We have some rather *good* news for you, don't we, Miss Hardbroom?'

'We certainly do,' said Miss Hardbroom. 'You see, Mildred, it would seem to us, that the marked difference in your flying skill is down to the fact that you now have a broom-companion with natural ability.'

'And we have also noticed,' said Miss Cackle, 'that your tabby cat – yes, I *know* he is a sweet little thing,' she added, seeing the alarm on Mildred's face, 'but he's not doing you any favours, Mildred. The Grand High Witch herself explained that it's perfectly acceptable for a witch to have *any* animal on her broomstick, so we have decided to alter the time-honoured tradition of cats at this academy and allow you to have Star as your broomstick-companion. What do you say, Mildred?'

'But what about Tabby?' asked Mildred anxiously. 'I can't just send him away; he needs me, Miss Cackle – and I need him. He's my best cat – he's my *only* cat!'

'You don't *have* to send him away, my dear,' said Miss Cackle. 'There is no reason at all why you shouldn't keep them both: Star for broomstick duties and Tabby for doing what he likes best – let's face it – staying in your room in the warm and avoiding flying at all costs! *Now*, what do you say?'

'Oh, *thank* you, Miss Cackle!' exclaimed Mildred. 'That would be so wonderful, I can't think of anything better!'

'Off you go then, Mildred,' said Miss Cackle, rising from her chair. 'You can go and tell all your friends the good news.'

Mildred and Star were halfway out of the door when Miss Hardbroom stopped

them. 'Wait a moment,' she said, lifting a new Lantern Monitor's holdall from behind the desk, 'don't forget the lanterns tonight, Mildred – we still need to see where we're going, even if our best lantern-lighter *is* the school heroine of the moment. And I've had a word with Ethel and asked her to keep to her own side of the school, so there won't be any trouble.'

'Thank you *so* much, Miss Hardbroom,' said Mildred fervently. 'I promise I won't let you down.'

'And, Mildred,' added Miss Cackle pleasantly, 'no more strays, all right? I think that a cat, a dog, a tortoise *and* a colony of bats are quite enough to cram into one small room – any more and you'll need an extension!'

CHAPTER TWENTY-SIX

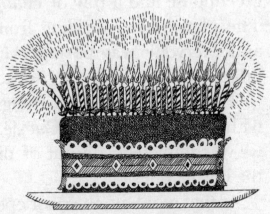

One day, a few weeks after the competition, the teachers were in the staffroom at morning break, excitedly discussing the swimming pool, which was at the planning stage. For a while, no one had been able to think of a place to put it as the school was perched on top of a mountain. In the end they decided on a back yard (called the Small Playground), which was only used occasionally for individual broomstick lessons. Miss Cackle had just received the architect's plans, beautifully drawn out, showing the pool with a glass roof like a greenhouse and a row of changing rooms. The plan looked thrilling from all angles and everyone was poring over it on the table, clutching their mugs of tea.

'I wish we'd got something nice to go with our tea,' said Miss Cackle. 'I'm afraid we've completely run out of biscuits, even the boring ones.'

At that moment, the door opened and, to everyone's astonishment, Miss Hardbroom came into the room, her face glowing in the light of a candle-covered cake. She carried it over to the table and set it down very carefully for everyone to admire, Miss Drill surreptitiously attempting to count the candles, so she could work out how old Miss Hardbroom was.

'What's all this, Miss Hardbroom?' asked Miss Cackle, who couldn't help noticing the chocolate cake underneath the candles.

'It's my birthday today,' announced Miss Hardbroom, 'and I thought it was about time I had a proper cake, so that we could all have a slice with our morning cup of tea.'

'What a splendid idea, Miss Hardbroom!' agreed Miss Cackle fervently.

Miss Hardbroom took a deep breath and blew out all the candles in one go. Everyone clapped politely.

'Did you make a wish, Miss Hardbroom?' asked Miss Cackle, as they busied themselves removing the candles and cutting up the cake.

'Oh really, Miss Cackle,' laughed Miss Hardbroom, handing the headmistress an extra-large slice. 'As if anyone actually believes in all that silly nonsense.'

Mildred Hubble is always getting her spells
wrong at Miss Cackle's Academy for Witches.
But she manages to get by until she turns Ethel,
the teacher's pet, into her deadly enemy . . .

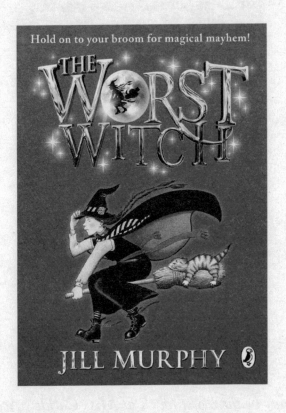

The first in the much-loved Worst Witch series

puffin.co.uk

What happens when disaster-prone
Mildred Hubble meets new girl Enid Nightshade?

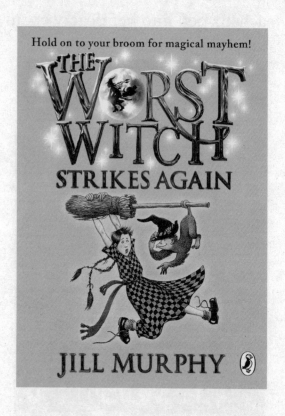

*She may be the worst witch at Miss Cackle's Academy
for Witches, but she's the best friend you could ever have!*

puffin.co.uk

A new term, and Mildred is determined to
lose her reputation as the worst witch
Miss Cackle's Academy has ever seen –
but things get rapidly out of hand.

*Millions of readers love Mildred Hubble –
and so will you . . .*

Mildred stows away her beloved cat, Tabby,
on a class trip to the seaside. Trying to keep him out
of sight of Miss Hardbroom leads her from one
disaster to another, and soon she really is all at sea.

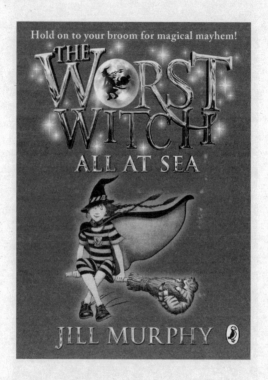

'Hurray for Jill Murphy . . . girls will love the
antics of Mildred Hubble and her
hopeless tabby cat' – *Independent*

puffin.co.uk

A new teacher, a hair-growth spell gone wrong and a cat who refuses to fly – can Mildred overcome all obstacles and save the day?

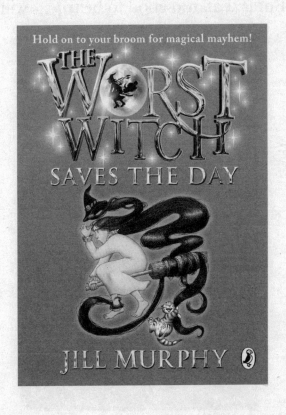

'A lovely, sparkly book' – *Observer*

puffin.co.uk

Mildred's done the best holiday project ever
and she's sure Miss Hardbroom will be impressed.
Even her arch-enemy, Ethel Hallow, is being friendly
to her! But is it all too good to be true – will disaster
strike again for the Worst Witch?

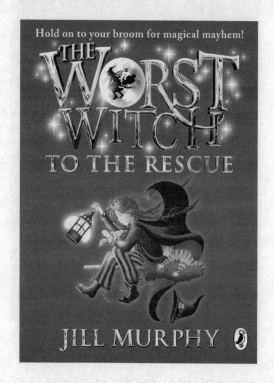

'Readers can't fail to warm to Mildred Hubble'
– *Booktrust*

puffin.co.uk

Get to know Mildred Hubble
from her very first disastrous day!

She may be the worst witch at Miss Cackle's Academy for Witches, but she's the best friend you could ever have.

It all started with a Scarecrow

Puffin is over seventy years old.
Sounds ancient, doesn't it? But Puffin has never been
so lively. We're always on the lookout for the next big
idea, which is how it began all those years ago.

Penguin Books was a big idea from the mind of
a man called Allen Lane, who in 1935 invented
the quality paperback and changed the world.
**And from great Penguins, great Puffins grew,
changing the face of children's books forever.**

The first four Puffin Picture Books were hatched in 1940 and the
first Puffin story book featured a man with broomstick arms called
Worzel Gummidge. In 1967 Kaye Webb, Puffin Editor, started the
Puffin Club, promising to **'make children into readers'**.
She kept that promise and over 200,000 children became devoted
Puffineers through their quarterly instalments of *Puffin Post*.

Many years from now, we hope you'll look back and
remember Puffin with a smile. **No matter what your age
or what you're into, there's a Puffin for everyone.**
The possibilities are endless, but one thing is for sure:
whether it's a picture book or a paperback, a sticker book
or a hardback, **if it's got that little Puffin
on it – it's bound to be good.**

www.puffin.co.uk